W9-AFS-704

BITSY AND THE MYSTERY AT TYBEE ISLAND

VONDA SKINNER SKELTON

MYSTERIES
An Imprint of The Overmountain Press
JOHNSON CITY, TENNESSEE

Book design by Cherisse McGinty

Hardcover ISBN 1-57072-253-6
Trade Paper ISBN 1-57072-254-4
Copyright © 2003 by Vonda Skinner Skelton
Printed in the United States of America
All Rights Reserved

1 2 3 4 5 6 7 8 9 0

For my precious daughters,
Christina Skelton Hunt
and
Nicole Skelton Matheny

ACKNOWLEDGMENTS

Thank you to my daughters, Christina and Nicole, and to my friends Carrie, Danielle, and Leah Whiddon, Cathy Strawhorn, and Ellis Vidler for their proofreading and editorial input,

To the late A. P. Smith and Ann Smith for an informative and entertaining afternoon of background information,

To the Tybee Island Historical Society for valuable historic input,

To my parents, Ruth Skinner Poole and the late Bob Skinner, and my sisters and brother, Gail, Laura, and Scott, who gave me a childhood of endless adventure,

To my mother for research assistance,

To Beth, Sherry, Karin, and the rest of the Silver Dagger family for your guidance, encouragement, and commitment,

And to the love of my life, my husband, Gary, for always being my Number One Fan.

C H A P T E R · 1

"HE IS, TOO!"

"He ain't, either!"

"He is, too!"

"He ain't, either!" I screamed back at my little sister.

Grief! Why in the world did Mother and Daddy want so many kids? It was peaceful and calm and quiet and easy when it was just me. Now I have to deal with two bratty sisters plus another kid on the way.

I glared down at Ann with her grimy little hand on her hip, tapping her dirty, bare foot. It's amazing how someone so small can make your life so miserable.

She balled her fists, stretched up on her tiptoes, and screeched at the top of her lungs, "He is, too!"

I'd had enough. I bent over her, stared into those squinty blue eyes, and growled through my teeth, "He . . . ain't . . . either."

We were eyeball-to-eyeball, nose-to-nose. Her hot breath hit me in the face, but I didn't blink.

"Bitsy, what's going on in here?" my mother yelled as

she came through the back door with her empty laundry basket.

Now, correct me if I'm wrong here, but weren't there *two* kids in this argument?

I stood up real straight and held myself as tall as I could. "Ann says that Bobby Crumley is my boyfriend, and he ain't."

"He isn't," Mother said.

I turned to Ann and smirked. "See, I told you so."

"No, Bitsy," my mother corrected. "You said 'ain't,' and it should be 'isn't.' Now y'all stop all this fussing and set the table for supper."

I looked at my mother and didn't say a word. *Is that it? Just "Now y'all set the table for supper?" How about an apology from Ann? Is that too much to ask around here? Grief!*

I climbed up on the counter and pulled down five chipped plates from the cabinet. I wanted to ask my mother what was the big deal about setting the table anyway. It's not like we have a real supper. It's not like we have real food. But I kept my mouth shut.

As I set the plates on the table, Mother sliced the fatback and threw it in the frying pan, just like she had done for the past three days. I watched the sweat trickle down her face and wondered if she was as tired of fatback and honey buns as I was.

Mother says we should just thank the good Lord that we have food to eat. She says there are poor kids who don't have any food at all. Now, don't get me wrong, I thank God every day for the greasy fatback and old honey buns. But I certainly wouldn't mind it if He decided to send some pizza my way. Hey, maybe on that day I could send my fatback and honey bun to the poor kids!

Anyway, Ann plopped down in front of the TV and started watching "Sesame Street" with my baby sister, Lynn, while I did all the work. But I wasn't complaining. At least they weren't bugging me, for once. I looked across the room at Ann and wondered how we could possibly be sisters. I guess you could say we're complete opposites.

I'm always the shortest person in my class; that's why they call me Bitsy—my real name is Elizabeth Ruth Burroughs. I have short brown hair that's real curly, and brown eyes, and a big dimple right in the middle of my chin, just like my daddy. I'm not the least bit shy, and I can beat up any guy my age. I've done it lots of times. I'm the only girl in the whole softball league, and most of my friends are guys.

And then there's Ann. Her real name is Margaret Ann, after my Aunt Margaret. But Mother didn't want to have two Margarets in the family, so we just call my sister Ann. Anyway, like I said, she's not at all like me. She's kinda tall for her age, has straight blonde hair, and those squinty blue eyes. She's real shy and doesn't like to be with other people. I wish she didn't like to be with me, but she sure seems to be hanging around all the time. And believe me, a twelve-year-old does not want a six-year-old hanging around.

Now, my baby sister, Lynn, isn't as much trouble. Maybe it's because she's just three and hasn't learned how to aggravate me yet. Or maybe it just doesn't seem like she's as much trouble since she looks exactly like me. But she's still a bratty little sister. Her name is Lynn Jeannine. Mother wanted to have a redheaded daughter, but Lynn ended up looking just like me and Daddy.

And then there's the new one. I couldn't believe it when Mother told me we were going to have another baby. Why would anybody want four kids? Especially since Mother and Daddy always say we don't have enough money. When she told me there was going to be another one, I asked her where the money was going to come from to pay for it. I even reminded her of that awful day when me and Ann and Lynn had to hide in her bedroom while that bill collector was banging on the front door.

He was yelling, "I know you're in there, Mrs. Burroughs. And you know you're three months late on your payment!" It was really scary for the little kids, but I knew I could protect us if I had to.

Anyway, Mother said that money isn't everything and that they were very thankful for the new baby, even if I wasn't. Then she told me she hoped it was another girl so we could have a Burroughs Sisters Quartet. She keeps saying she wants us to sing on TV like the Lemon Sisters, whoever they are. Can you believe it? Me singing with my bratty sisters? Now, don't get me wrong. I love to sing, and I'm great on stage. But personally, I'd rather just have a baby brother and sing by myself on TV.

Supper that night was like every other night, with Ann and Lynn making their usual racket while we asked God to bless the food, and their usual mess while we ate it all up. And, as usual, Daddy didn't get home in time to eat with us.

See, my daddy drives a bread truck, which means he delivers bread to all the stores and restaurants around town. It's a hard job and he works long hours, but at least we get the old bread and honey buns for free. Daddy says this job really does put food on the table. And I always laugh when he says it, even though I've heard him say it at least a thousand times.

"Nine o'clock, girls," my mother announced as "The Waltons" rerun ended. "Time for bed."

"Please let me stay up till Daddy gets home," I begged.

"Me, too!" cried Ann.

"Me, too!" echoed Lynn.

But my mother didn't back down. "No. I said it's time for bed, and that's what I mean."

Now, I have to give my mother credit here. She says what she means and she means what she says. So when Mother says, "Time for bed," that's it. No amount of begging or pleading or tantrum-throwing will get her to change her mind. But sometimes I just have to give it a try. And this was one of those times. I needed to see my daddy.

I decided to try the adult approach. I didn't cry. I didn't even whine. I just said, real grown-up-like, "Mother, please let me stay up. I'm too big to go to bed the same time the little kids do." Now, that was a mature statement if I've ever heard one.

"Yes, Bitsy, you're right. You really should be able to stay up later. But to be honest, I need you to go to bed early tonight. I need the peace and quiet."

She needs the peace and quiet? *She* needs the peace and quiet? I'm the one who has to live in a tiny bedroom with wall-to-wall beds holding wall-to-wall kids! I'm the one who'll have to put up with a bawling baby in the crib and Ann and Lynn sharing the bunk below me. I'm the one who has to put up with kids getting into my stuff. Why can't some of these kids go sleep in *her* room where they can bother *her* stuff? Grief!

So much for adult conversation.

Fifteen minutes later I was lying in bed, feeling sorry for myself and listening to the endless *slurp-slurp-slurp* of my two thumb-sucking sisters. Then I remembered the box, the big cardboard box under the crib.

You see, Daddy is always working extra jobs or inventing new gadgets in order to make more money for our family. His latest business was filling bubble gum machines, and a year's supply of gum balls was hidden in the box under the crib.

I was the only one who knew it was there. The day I found it, Daddy explained that there was no other place in our little house to put the box, and he would just have to trust me not to eat up all his profits. He didn't say I couldn't have any, he just said there were a few rules attached.

First of all, I could only chew one piece a day. Second of all, I couldn't go to sleep with gum in my mouth. And third of all, I had to brush my teeth after I finished the gum. I followed the rules almost every day.

But that night I imagined a crunchy red ball rolling around my mouth and could even taste the sweet juice as it ran all over my tongue. The temptation was more than I could bear. "I'll brush my teeth twice as long tomorrow," I promised God.

I climbed down from my top bunk, quietly opened the lid of the box, and reached my hand into the secret stash of bubble gum balls. My heart was pounding like a jackhammer as I waved my fingers back and forth through the round goodies. In the darkness, I selected the perfect gum ball, pulled it out of the box, and placed it between my teeth. Just as I crunched the gum in two, I heard the screen door creak open. Daddy was home!

I threw the gum into the trash can and ran the few steps from my bedroom to the living room. "Daddy!" I jumped into his arms just as Mother was waking up on the couch.

"I'm glad you're still awake, Bitsy," he said, grinning from ear to ear.

I turned to Mother and smiled. I wanted to say, *See, I knew Daddy wanted me to stay up.* But I didn't say anything.

Daddy continued, "I have some good news!"

Mother pulled herself up, and Daddy patted the couch for me to sit beside him. His brown eyes were sparkling as he proudly said, "Guess what. We're going on a vacation!"

I jumped up and down. "A vacation! We've never had a vacation before!"

Daddy stood and held out his arms for Mother's hug.

But Mother was already arguing. "Robert, you know we can't afford a vacation. How can you even suggest such nonsense?"

He sat down. "Well, Ruth, that's the first exciting part. We *can* afford it!"

My mother couldn't believe what she was hearing. "What are—?"

"At work today they announced the Salesman of the Quarter. And guess who got it? Me!"

I jumped up and down. Daddy stood and held out his arms again. But Mother wasn't giving up that easy.

"I'm very proud of you, Robert," she said. "But what does that have to do with us going on vacation?"

I stopped jumping. Daddy sat back down on the couch.

"That's the second exciting part," he said. "Along with the award, I also got a hundred-dollar bonus!"

I jumped up and down again. Daddy stood and held out his arms.

But no hug was coming from Mother. "Honey, that's great," she said. "But a hundred dollars won't pay for a vacation."

I stopped jumping. Daddy plopped back down on the couch.

"That's the third exciting part," he said. "There's a man at work, I think you've met him—Mr. Mull?"

Mother stared at Daddy. She didn't say anything.

"Well, anyway, he said we could use his cabin at Tybee Island, Georgia, for only twenty dollars for the whole week. And it's right on the beach!"

I didn't jump up and down this time. I watched my mother and waited. But Daddy stood again and held out his arms.

"Twenty dollars?" she whispered.

He had her! My mother could always appreciate a good bargain. At last she ran into Daddy's arms. I jumped up and down.

Daddy continued with the plans. "After the twenty dollars for the cabin, we'll still have eighty dollars to buy gas and food while we're there."

Food? Did Daddy say "food"?

"Do you mean real food like you buy in the grocery store?" I asked.

"Yep! No stale honey buns or fried fatback for this family for a whole week! We'll even go out to eat one night at the famous Williams Seafood Restaurant!"

"Hot dog!" I yelled. "When do we get to go?"

"Next week."

"Next week?" Mother said. "Robert, you know we can't go until after the baby is born. It's too close to time."

"But, Ruth, next week is the only time the cabin is available. And the baby isn't due for another month. If it will make you feel better, I'll find us a doctor as soon as we get there, just in case. But it's next week or not at all."

I looked at Daddy. I looked at Mother. Don't tell me this kid is going to mess up my life before it's even born!

"Okay," Mother said. "Just remember, it's a vacation for me, too."

"Uh, one other thing," Daddy said. "I've developed a suntan lotion—"

"A suntan lotion? Robert, what in the world do you know about suntan lotion?"

"That's not the point. Look, everybody's buying some kind of lotion and getting a suntan. And what about this stuff called Bronzetone? Do you know what's in it? Nothing but lanolin and mineral oil and a few other things. And somebody's making a million! It might as well be me!"

"But, Robert—"

"Don't you see, Ruth? This could be our year to make it big."

"But, Robert—" Mother tried again, more forcefully.

"No 'buts,'" Daddy said. "I've already decided. My lotion is called TanTone. And we'll test it at the beach!"

C H A P T E R · 2

THAT NIGHT I was so excited I could hardly sleep. We were really going to the beach! I was lying in bed, imagining all the fun we would have, when suddenly it hit me: I would be alone at the beach. Mother and Daddy would be together, Ann and Lynn would be together, but I wouldn't have anybody. Actually, I would rather be alone than hang around the little kids, but that wasn't the point.

So the next morning I asked Mother if I could invite my cousin Matt to go with us. He's a few months younger than me, but a lot taller. He's a great softball player, and, best of all, he doesn't treat me like a sissy old girl.

Mother didn't like my idea at all. "Why would I want another child to go? What kind of vacation would that be for me?" she asked no one in particular. "Another mouth to feed, more bodies to keep up with, more—"

"Mother, please! I'll be so lonely! What kind of vacation would that be for me?"

"I'm sorry, Bitsy. I understand what you're saying. But

we can't do it. We just can't afford it."

I stomped out of the living room and headed toward the tiny bedroom. I didn't believe for one minute that she was really sorry, and I was sure she didn't understand.

By the time I reached my room, a part of me wanted to yell and slam the door and throw something. But I knew that making a scene wouldn't get me anywhere. So I came up with a better idea.

You see, Mother always tells me that the way to get along with difficult people is to "kill 'em with kindness." Since she was definitely being a difficult person, I took her advice.

There wasn't a pen or a piece of paper in my room, so I used a red crayon and wrote on the back of an envelope.

My Dearest Mother,

I know it was a lot to ask to let Matt go with us. And I'm sorry I acted the way I did. But after thinking about the situation, I really don't feel like I will fit in at the beach with the rest of the family. So maybe it would be better if I just don't go on vacation this time. It might work out better for me next time. That is, if we ever get to go to the beach again.

143,

Elizabeth Ruth Burroughs (Bitsy)

Just so you know, the "143" means "I love you." See, *I* has one letter, *love* has four letters, and *you* has three letters. It's a secret code my parents had when they were dating, and now our family uses it all the time.

Anyway, it worked! It really worked! Mother finally admitted that it might be lonely for me without a buddy, and she said I could invite Matt. This would be the best vacation anybody could ever have. Real food, the beach, and my favorite cousin, Matt.

The car trunk was packed with suitcases we borrowed from our relatives. But I had all my good stuff in the special bag my Grandma Burroughs brought me last year from Cherokee, North Carolina. See, my daddy's great-grandmother was a full-blooded Cherokee Indian, and my grandmother wants to make sure we don't forget it. She doesn't have to worry about me. I will never forget it. I'm proud of every single drop of my Cherokee blood. And all my friends think it's really cool that I'm part Indian. That's where me and Daddy and Lynn get our dark hair and brown eyes.

Anyway, Grandma gave each of us vacation treats—a puzzle book, pencils, crayons, paper, scissors, and sun-glasses. Of course, Ann and Lynn lost theirs before we even left for the beach, but I put all my stuff in the Cherokee bag and then filled the pockets with bubble gum. I figured Daddy wouldn't be worried about bubble gum profits when he strikes it rich with TanTone suntan lotion.

It was barely light outside when we left that Monday morning at six o'clock. Thank goodness, Matt was with me for the long ride from Greenville, South Carolina, to Tybee Island, Georgia. We looked for different state tags on cars and talked in Pig Latin and had bubble-gum-blowing contests. I couldn't have had nearly as much fun with Ann and Lynn.

And since the air conditioner was broken, we fought constantly with my sisters over who got to sit by the windows and feel the wind. But all in all, it wasn't too bad. At least I had Matt.

It was getting close to lunchtime when we got there. "Here it is!" Daddy said as we pulled in front of a white cement block cabin. We climbed out of the car to look at our home away from home for the next seven days.

It looked like a cool cabin, but what caught my eye was the old building next to ours. I ran ahead to take a closer look and couldn't believe what I found. There it was, right beside our cabin—a real military fort with steps and bars and darkened doorways. "A fort!" I shouted.

Matt and I were headed to it, when Daddy yelled, "Hey, where do you two think you're going? Get back over here and unload the car."

"But, Daddy—"

"Look, kids, we're here to play in the sand and ride the waves and test my TanTone. We're not here to wander through some musty old building."

"But, Daddy, aren't you curious about it? I wonder how old it is. Do you think it was built during the Civil War?"

"I don't know. I'm sure we'll find out all about it while we're here this week. But first things first. You two help empty the car so your mother can lie down. It's been an especially long ride for her. Poor thing, she can hardly move."

I knew the only way we were going to ever get into the fort was to do as Daddy said and unload the car. But first we had to help him check out the cabin.

We found the entrance on the side of the cabin. The screen door was tilted, barely held on by one hinge at the top. Daddy gently lifted the door open, scraping the bottom on the sidewalk. He went in first and started opening windows to let in some fresh air. I opened the back door in the kitchen as Mother herded the little ones in through the side.

The place wasn't the Hilton, but it sure looked good to me. I actually thought we had a pretty good deal for twenty bucks. There were two bedrooms full of furniture that didn't match. The kitchen didn't have any hot water, and there were crumbs all over the cement floor, but the table was big enough for all of us to gather around. And last but not least, there was a bathroom with an open shower right smack in the middle of the room. There wasn't even a shower curtain.

Mother ran us out of the bathroom so she could use it first. We were headed back out to unpack the car when I heard the loudest scream I've ever heard in my entire life.

"ROBERT!" It was my mother!

I turned and ran back toward the bathroom. I was rounding the corner from the kitchen when I saw something furry scamper through the torn screen of the back door. I kept my eyes on the strange creature but continued to run toward the bathroom.

Bam! I never knew what hit me as I collided with my mother's big belly. I landed hard on the cement floor, but Mother never missed a beat. Screaming at the top of her lungs, this woman (the poor thing who could hardly move) sailed over me like a hurdler, ran through the cluttered bedroom, and dashed out the screen door, crashing it to the sidewalk.

She never looked back. So much for maternal instinct.

By the time I picked myself up and got outside, Mother had stopped screaming, but she was still shaking.

"A rat!" she yelled. "There was a rat in the toilet! It climbed up my back when I sat down! I'm never going back in there. I want to go home! Now, Robert, now!"

Ann and Lynn held on to Mother's legs and cried.

Well, if Daddy thought convincing Mother to *come* to the beach was hard, then convincing her to *stay* was even harder. Matt and I had to help Daddy go over the entire cabin with a broom and look for the frightened creature. We even moved every stick of dirty furniture. Finally, Mother agreed that the animal I saw running out the kitchen door must have been the bathroom rat. She wasn't excited about it, but she let us help her and the little ones into bed for a nap, then we headed to the car to unpack it.

First, I carried in my special bag. Matt and I hid it behind a wooden chest so the little kids couldn't find it.

Then we started back for the next load. Walking on the sidewalk back to the car, I realized just how close that fort really was.

"Look, Matt. There's the door, just a few steps from the sidewalk. It won't hurt to take a quick peek inside."

"I don't know, Bitsy. You know what your daddy said."

"Aw, come on. I'm not talking about taking the grand tour, you know. I just want to look in the door."

"Well, I guess it's okay," Matt said. "It is only three or four steps away."

We looked back toward the open doorway of the cabin, the screen door still stretched out on the sidewalk. Daddy was busy unpacking suitcases, and Mother and the girls were asleep. We looked at each other and smiled.

"We can go right through this door," I whispered as I quietly stepped onto the white sand.

Matt tiptoed behind me. "I wonder if anybody has been inside here since it was used as a real fort. Maybe we're the first ones to explore it in years."

"Shhh! Do you want Daddy to hear us?"

Matt didn't answer, but he followed me as we took five baby steps into the fort.

The damp, dark room was totally silent. A slight breeze blew against my back. I stopped. I shivered from the coolness of the fort. Or was it from the creepy feeling I suddenly had in the pit of my stomach? I decided I wasn't so interested in the fort after all.

"Matt, we better go. I . . . uh . . . I don't want Daddy to find us in here."

Matt cleared his throat. "Yeah. Me, neither."

We turned back toward the entrance. And there he was. I stopped a scream by covering my mouth with both hands, but Matt just stood there with his jaw hanging open.

I wanted to run. I needed to escape. But I couldn't get out. The doorway was blocked by a huge, dark man! And I knew immediately that he was evil. His eyes were like big, inky holes glaring right through us, reading our souls. He didn't utter a sound. His black beard was so bushy, I wasn't even sure he had a mouth!

He stood there only a few seconds, but it seemed like forever. He looked at us. We looked at him. Nobody said a word. He turned and walked away, but his eyes stayed glued to us until he was gone.

I stood frozen in the empty room, afraid to move, afraid to speak. Matt, his mouth still hanging open, was barely breathing.

"Matt!" I whispered.

He didn't answer.

"Matt!" I whispered louder. "Let's get out of here!"

I ran for the door, with Matt right behind me. We looked up and down the sidewalk and behind the fort, but we couldn't find the evil-looking man anywhere. The only people we saw were two men on a porch across the street.

We sat down hard on the sidewalk and rested against the cabin. We were still huffing and puffing.

"Well, what do you think?" I asked between breaths.

"I think we need to stay out of the fort," Matt said, his voice shaking.

I cleared my throat. "Oh, I'm sure it was nothing. He was probably just as surprised to see us as we were to see him."

"Uh, yeah. I guess you're right."

I stood up, reached down for my cousin's hand, and pulled him to his feet. "Come on. We're wasting time here. Let's finish unpacking the car so we can get to the beach."

Matt smiled.

But as we walked back to the car, I started feeling kind of sad. I wanted to tell Daddy about the evil-looking man and how scared I was, but I couldn't because we weren't supposed to be in the fort in the first place. That meant I had to keep a secret from my daddy. And Daddy and I don't believe in keeping secrets from each other.

It's amazing how much stuff it takes to handle two adults and four kids for a whole week. After a zillion trips back and forth to the car, we finally had everything inside.

By this time Mother and the girls were feeling much better and were ready to go to the ocean. We gobbled down lunch, and everyone started getting dressed for the beach. Everyone, that is, except Daddy. He had to keep his promise to Mother and find the nearest doctor, just in case she decided to have that baby early. He also had to buy new hinges for the broken door. But before he left, he gave us the TanTone test instructions.

"First, put TanTone on your right side. Then put Bronzetone on your left. And don't forget to put it on again every time you come out of the water."

Ann raised her hand and jumped up and down. "Daddy! Daddy! I have a 'portant question."

Daddy smiled as he patted her blonde head. "Yes, what is it?"

"Is my front side or my back side the right side?"

Daddy chuckled as he picked up the two little girls. "Bitsy and Matt will help you. Now y'all hurry and get to the beach so we can start the test. The sooner we can prove how good it is, the sooner we'll be rich!"

Well, believe me, it was no fun getting those two little kids dressed. Nobody could find what they needed to wear, and nobody wanted to wear what they could find. After arguing over bathing suits, sandals, and toys, we finally had everybody ready.

We had only taken a few steps around the broken door when Matt grabbed my arm. "Bitsy, look! Over the top of the fort—is that a lighthouse?"

I turned to the direction Matt was pointing, while Ann and Lynn pushed their way around Mother to get a good look.

"It is!" I said. "And it's just a few streets over from here."

Matt shook his head in amazement. "Man, a fort *and* a lighthouse! Is this the greatest place, or what?"

"Can we go see it today, Mother?" I asked. "Please? Please?"

"No," Mother said, placing her hand on her hip. "Can't we please just go to the beach? That is what we're here for, you know."

Nobody said a word while Mother looked down at each one of us. None of us had the nerve to argue.

"Good," she said. "Now, let's go."

We headed down the steaming sidewalk. I watched Matt glance over at the fort and then turn to me. We stopped and stared at the empty doorway. Memories of the evil-looking man flooded my brain, and I shivered again.

"What's the holdup, Bitsy?" Mother called.

"Oh, nothing. Sorry." I put Lynn on my hip and started again. Matt got the hint and picked up Ann. Mother waddled behind us as the sidewalk ended, and we all took the path to the beach.

I had never seen so much water in my whole life. We plopped the little ones down and ran to the edge of the waves. As far as I could see was water—warm, salty, fishy water. It was a thousand times bigger than any lake back home in South Carolina.

But looking at the ocean wasn't gonna make us rich. I headed back toward the beach bag. "Come on! Let's get started!" I pulled out the old baby bottle full of greasy TanTone and grabbed the fancy orange tube of Bronze-tone. We put the lotion on just like Daddy said—Tan-Tone on the right, and Bronzetone on the left. Then we slathered up the little kids.

We all raced back to the water and had a blast riding

the waves to the shore. When we got tired of the water, Mother showed us how to build a sandcastle. Finally we just stretched out in the sun and let the TanTone work.

I was almost asleep, and Matt was on a towel beside me, when I heard someone walk up. Visions of the evil-looking man filled my brain as my eyes snapped open.

I was surprised to see two men standing over us, their backs to the sun.

They smiled. "Hey," they said together.

"Uh, hello," I answered as I slowly sat up. My eyes scanned the waves and found Mother close by with the girls. She was watching us.

"Hi," Matt added.

"I'm Billy Smith," the shorter one said. "And this here's Tim Nelson. We're in the cabin across the road from you."

"Oh, yeah," I said. "We saw you a while ago when we came out of the fo—"

Matt interrupted me. "We saw you a while ago on your porch. I'm Matt." He turned to me. "And this is my cousin Bitsy. Nice to meet you."

"Yeah. You, too," Mr. Smith said. "We're here on vacation. You gonna be here long?"

"No, sir, just this week," I said. "Mr. Mull is letting us use his cabin."

Mr. Smith laughed. "'No, sir?' Nobody ain't never said 'sir' to me." He elbowed Mr. Nelson. "Ain't that nice?"

Mr. Nelson nodded his head in agreement. I noticed a black hole where his front teeth should have been.

Mr. Smith turned back to us. "But you don't have to say 'sir' to us. We ain't no better than you. Just call me Billy and him Tim." Then he scanned the area around us, leaned down, and whispered, "By the way, we seen y'all going in that old fort back there."

My eyes must have opened really wide, because he added, "Oh, don't worry. We won't tell nobody. But you just might want to be careful. You know, it could be dangerous in there."

"Boy, that's the truth!" I blurted out. Then Matt and I told them all about the evil-looking man.

"And we never could find him when we ran out," I said. "But we know he was up to no good. You could tell just by looking at him. He really looked evil."

"I know what you mean," Billy said. "Me and Tim seen him yesterday. You're right. He is weird. I think I'd stay out of that fort if I was you."

I smiled but didn't say anything else. I wasn't about to promise them we'd stay out of the fort.

"Mind if we join you?" Billy asked.

"No, sir . . . I mean, no," I answered. It was hard not to say "sir" to a grown-up.

Billy and Tim sat down on the sand beside us and started their own sandcastle. We got up to help. At first I was hoping they had some kids we could play with. But after a while, I realized we could have fun with them. They weren't like most grown-ups.

Soon Mother and the girls came up, and I introduced them to our new friends. After they talked for a few minutes, we all decided to build a sandcastle, and we built the best one you've ever seen. It had a moat with a bridge made out of a paper plate and a tower almost as tall as Lynn.

We told Billy and Tim about Daddy's TanTone experiment, and they told us how to catch crabs. Tim even went back to their cabin and got some wieners to go crabbing with. I couldn't believe it. Here they were, feeding perfectly good wieners to the crabs, while we had to eat old honey buns and fatback at home.

Anyway, we ended up catching eleven crabs that afternoon. Mother had never cooked crabs and didn't want to learn how, so we gave them all to our new friends.

While Billy and Tim were packing up the catch, Daddy came running down the path, shouting to Mother that he had found a doctor. "His name's Dr. Shaw, and he's right here on the island, just a mile or so away. Said he'd be glad to help if we needed him this week." Then Daddy laughed and said, "Of course, if you want someone even closer, the veterinarian, Dr. Verdin, is only one street over!"

"Very funny!" my mother said, trying to act annoyed. "Very funny!"

Then she turned to our new friends. "Robert, I want you to meet Billy and Tim. They're vacationing in the cabin across the street."

Daddy stuck out his hand. "Nice to meet you."

"You, too," they answered together.

Billy shook Daddy's hand and then said, "Well, we hate

to run, but we better get to work on these-here crabs." Billy picked up the bucket, and Tim followed him up the path.

"Come back and see us," Daddy called after them.

"Sure thing," Billy answered. "We'll do that."

Daddy turned back to Mother. "I've got some bad news. We may not be able to eat at Williams Seafood after all. The headlines in the paper said they were robbed yesterday, and the restaurant was still closed when I came by this afternoon."

"Oh, no!" Mother and I said together.

But Mother was the first to actually whine. "Does that mean I have to cook every single night we're here? I thought this was supposed to be my vacation."

I figured it was okay to whine if Mother did. "Daddy, you mean we don't get to go to a real restaurant?"

He patted my head and put his arm around my mother. "Well, we'll see what we can do," Daddy said. Then he turned to the little ones. "Okay, kiddos, time to head back for supper. Besides, I've got to get that screen door fixed tonight." He smiled at Matt and me and whispered loudly, "I'd hate for another creature to get in the house."

"Robert, that's not even funny!" Mother said as she punched his arm.

He gave her one of his big bear hugs and tried to be serious. "You're right, Ruth, it wasn't funny. But you have to admit. . . ."

Then Daddy couldn't help it. He started laughing that

little laugh you make when you're trying so hard not to laugh at all. You know the kind I mean. And before we knew it, we all were bending over, holding our stomachs and laughing until we cried. Oh, how I love those laughs.

The sky was turning beautiful shades of pink and purple as we trudged back up the path, lugging my sisters and all their junk. With Mother slowly following behind us, Daddy examined our arms and legs and decided that TanTone had definitely tanned better than Bronzetone.

To tell you the truth, I wasn't so sure I could tell any difference. But I didn't say that to my daddy.

CHAPTER · 3

MATT AND I had planned to sleep late the next morning, but you-know-who messed up that great idea. Ann and Lynn were whining when they woke me up, because they finally realized we didn't have a TV at the beach. Big deal. They couldn't watch "Mister Rogers," and they thought it was the end of the world.

After thirty minutes of their racket, I couldn't take it anymore. I finally gave in and told them to wake up Matt. If I had to be up this early, so did he. I sat up in my bed and watched from across the room as Ann pulled a feather out of Matt's pillow and used it to tickle his nose. Lynn stood at the foot of the bed and giggled, happy to be part of the prank.

"Hey!" Matt yelled as he jumped out of bed and started chasing the girls. They squealed and took off running, jumping on the bed along the way.

"Be quiet!" I whispered loudly. "You'll wake up Mother and Daddy."

They stopped squealing but continued to chase each

other. I headed to the kitchen to find us some breakfast.

Over two bowls of imitation Frosted Flakes, Matt and I worked on our plans to check out the fort and the lighthouse. "At least this time we don't have to sneak around," he said. "And I won't be as scared, with your parents around."

"Oh, Matt, you're just being a chicken. I wasn't really scared yesterday. Were you?"

"Of . . . of course not. I was, uh, just tired after that long trip."

I looked right into my cousin's eyes and lied through my teeth, "Yeah, I was just tired, too."

By the time Mother and Daddy got up, Matt and I were chomping at the bit to get started. But, again, other plans had been made for us.

"A museum? A *museum*?" I whined to my mother. Okay, I admit it. Two whines in two days is a lot, but I wanted to go to the lighthouse and explore the fort. I *had* to do something. "Why do we have to go to a dumb ol' museum?"

But, as usual, Mother said what she meant and meant what she said. "Now, listen, it's not very often we're this close to such a wonderful collection of history. Besides, it'll be good for you."

Good for me? This is supposed to be a vacation! I didn't want something that was good for me. I wanted to have fun!

"Grief!" I cried, throwing myself on the tattered couch. It was a great piece of acting, if I must say so myself.

"Okay. It's your choice," Mother said. "You don't have to go if you don't want to, but . . ."

What? Was I hearing things? My mother had never changed her mind in her life. Hey, I could get good at this! My mind was going through all the benefits of being a good actress, when I realized Mother was still talking.

". . . so we'll just go without you. Maybe next time you'll be more considerate of other people and their feelings. You just stay put inside this cabin until we get back from the museum and lighthouse."

"You're going to the lighthouse, too?"

"Yes, Bitsy. Like I said, the lighthouse is part of the museum, so we'll be walking to both of them today."

"But I didn't know—"

"No 'buts,' young lady," Daddy interrupted. "You had your chance. Now, you just behave yourself while we're gone. Oh, and don't forget to lock the door."

I sat on the couch and pouted as my family walked out the door. I couldn't believe it—even Matt went with them.

My family's voices got farther and farther away as I sat on the couch with my arms crossed. Soon it was completely quiet. That's when I realized I was totally alone. Totally alone with the evil-looking man somewhere out there.

I jumped up from the couch and hooked the latch in place on the screen door. Then I slammed the wooden door and turned the key to lock it. But that wasn't enough. I slid the big armchair in front of the door.

Nobody could get in now.

For a while I worked puzzles and blew huge bubble gum bubbles. But about every minute, I looked out the window and listened for the evil-looking man.

Then I started feeling guilty. And I mean really guilty. Not the kind where "you know you'll get out of trouble if you act like you're sorry" guilty, but the honest stuff. The kind that makes you feel bad inside. I realized Mother and Daddy had gone to a lot of trouble to give us a special vacation, and I'd blown it.

I put away the puzzle book and spit out the gum. Then I knelt by the couch, folded my hands under my chin, and closed my eyes. It was time to get serious.

"Dear Lord, I'm sorry for acting like such a brat. Please forgive me. And, God, please help me not to get myself in a mess like this again."

Well, I did feel a little better. But something was still bothering me. It was something my third grade Sunday school teacher had taught me. Sitting now on the cabin floor, I could almost hear Mrs. Varner's sweet voice reading from the Bible, "Even a child is known by his doings."

I'll never forget what she said next: "That means that even though you're just a kid, you're still responsible for what you do. You're still responsible for your own actions. And you're still responsible for how they affect other people."

That meant there was no one to blame but me.

I got out the crayons, paper, and scissors from my Cherokee bag, then grabbed a pencil. I had to try to make up for my own actions.

I was hard at work when I heard heavy footsteps on the sidewalk outside the window. I held still and listened. There it was again! I raced to the other side of the room, squeezed myself behind the couch, and didn't breathe. This was worse than hiding from the bill collector!

I heard the screen door rattle as someone tried to open it. *It must be the evil-looking man!* I thought. *He's come to get me!*

"Bitsy!" a man's voice yelled.

"Matt!" another one called.

The voices sounded familiar. Slowly I pulled myself from behind the couch and crept to the window. Flattening my back against the wall, I stretched on my tiptoes and peeked out the window.

Their backs were turned to me, so I couldn't see their faces, but one was taller and skinnier than the other one.

What a relief! It was Billy and Tim, our friends from across the street. I pushed the heavy chair out of the way, turned the key, and jerked the door open. Our neighbors looked surprised to see me.

"Well, uh, how you doing, Bitsy?" Billy said. "We didn't think you was home."

Tim just nodded.

"Nobody's home but me," I said as I unlatched the screen door. "The others have gone to the museum and lighthouse. What're y'all doing?"

"Well," Tim said, "we was looking to see if anybody was—"

"We was just looking for you and Matt," Billy interrupted. "We wondered if y'all wanted to go crabbing again."

"Thanks for asking, but my family will be home soon, and I've got to finish something for my parents."

"Well, um, okay. If you're sure you don't want to go." Billy turned and began walking down the path to the beach. "Maybe we'll bring you back some crabs," he called over his shoulder.

"Okay, thanks. Bye." I closed the door, leaned against it, and took a deep breath of relief.

Then I remembered the locks. Quickly, I reopened the door, latched the screen, closed the door again and turned the lock. I pulled the armchair back in place for extra protection. After my heart quit pounding, which was about two minutes later, I got back to my project.

Time must have flown by, because soon I heard the excited chatter of my family as they ran up the sidewalk.

"Bitsy! Bitsy!" Matt yelled through the open window. "You're not going to believe what we saw."

I hid all my stuff behind the couch and ran to the door, moved the chair back to its place, and undid all the locks. Everybody tried to talk at the same time.

"The lighthouse had forty-leven steps!" Ann shouted. "And I walked all the way to the top!"

"You did not, Ann," Matt said. "Uncle Robert had to carry you. And it was a hundred and seventy-eight steps."

"Well, I still got to the top."

Matt laughed. "Okay, okay. You did get to the top."

Then he turned to me. "Bitsy, it was so cool. We found out they used to punish the drunk soldiers by making them march round and round the lighthouse carrying heavy weights on their backs."

"And we saw piwats, too!" Lynn said.

Everyone laughed except me.

"Piwats?" I asked.

"Pirates," Matt said. "We saw them at the museum."

I wasn't falling for that one. "You think I'm gonna believe there were pirates at the museum?"

"No. See, back in the 1700s, Blackbeard the Pirate was here, and—"

"The piwat was in this cabin?" Lynn broke in, wide-eyed.

"No," Matt answered. "Blackbeard was on this island, and he buried treasure here." He turned back to me. "We learned all about him at the museum."

I looked at Matt. This time *my* mouth was hanging open. "There's buried treasure on this island? On Tybee Island?"

Daddy cleared his throat. "Well now, I doubt that. See, that was almost three hundred years ago. There wouldn't be any way that there would—"

"What about the fort, then?" I asked. "Maybe he hid the treasure in the fort!"

"Nope. Couldn't happen," Matt answered. "See, the fort—it's called Battery Backus—was built in the 1890s, after the Civil War but before World War I. There are other forts all around us. They're all part of Fort Screven.

But anyway, the point is, the fort wasn't even here when Blackbeard was burying treasure."

"Grief!"

"And guess what else," Ann added, happy that she knew something else I didn't know.

"What?" I asked without interest.

"Our cabin was a bathroom. A 'ficial bathroom."

"A what?" I looked at Daddy. "What in the world is she talking about?"

Mother and Daddy laughed. Matt covered his mouth and snickered.

Daddy tried to get serious. "Well, it seems this lovely vacation home we are enjoying was once the Officers' Latrine of Fort Screven—the officers' bathroom," Daddy answered, losing control and laughing again.

"The bathroom? We're sleeping and eating in an old bathroom?" I stood up. "Grief!"

Mother and Daddy finally stopped laughing long enough to realize I was serious.

"What about germs?" I yelled as I paced back and forth. "What about diseases? What about infections?"

"Okay, okay," Mother said. "That's enough. We get the picture."

Daddy took over. "You have to remember, Bitsy, that was a long time ago. The place has been completely sanitized and cleaned since then. It had to be; otherwise, they wouldn't let someone live in it."

"Sure," I answered, without believing him. "Sure. That's why we have rats climbing out of the toilet!"

Now, I was confident Mother would be on my side after what she'd been through. I mean, after all, a rat had run up her back! But she just giggled at Daddy, and they both started laughing again, louder than ever.

I stopped pacing and just stood there. Then I turned away from my insensitive family. Tiptoeing to keep the germs off my bare feet, I passed Matt and entered the shabby bedroom. I could still hear them laughing as I put on my socks and shoes. Then I washed my hands. With soap and water. Three times.

C H A P T E R · 4

AFTER LUNCH I calmed down from my disgust over our cabin and decided to give Mother and Daddy my peace offering—a handmade card. I had drawn beautiful red and blue flowers on the front and written "I'M SORRY" on the inside.

I found my parents sitting in old lawn chairs behind the cabin. Mother opened the card and read it silently. She looked up at me, a tear sliding down her sunburned cheek.

Holding out her arms to me, she said, "Bitsy, that was so sweet. It makes me feel good to know that you really are sorry this time. I could tell this note came from your heart, not like the one you gave me about Matt coming to the beach with us."

"Uh, what do you mean?" I asked. But I knew what she meant.

"The note you gave me about Matt coming to the beach was written just to get what you wanted, wasn't it?"

I looked down at my feet.

"I knew it wasn't from your heart," Mother continued,

"but I also knew you had a point. You would be lonely. So Daddy and I decided to allow Matt to come, even though you didn't really deserve it. Then, when you pitched such a fit about the museum, well, it really hurt my feelings."

Daddy sat there, reading and rereading the card. He hadn't said a word, but I knew something painful was coming. Not painful like a spanking or being grounded, but the worst pain of all . . . knowing I had hurt my daddy.

He put the construction paper card on the chair and motioned for me to sit on his lap, my favorite place in the whole wide world. I snuggled up to him, and he put his arms around me. Then he took a deep breath.

"Bitsy, I think the part that hurt me the most was that you used our '143' to say something that wasn't true. I know we use it all the time, but it is very special to us. And to think you used it to try to trick us, well, that really disappointed me."

That's when I lost it. I cried for a long time while Daddy just held me close and smoothed my hair. After I had cried it all out, I slid off his lap.

With Mother and Daddy still in their chairs, I stood between them, my arms around their necks. "I'm so sorry. I promise to try to do better. And I promise that from now on, when I say '143,' I really do mean 'I Love You.'"

That afternoon Mother and Daddy offered to let Matt and me explore the fort while the rest of the family went to the beach. We were surprised when Daddy said we could skip the TanTone test. I think he felt sorry for me since I didn't get to go with them to the lighthouse.

We watched from the sidewalk as Daddy carried the little kids down the path, one on each hip. Mother was behind him, lugging the sand pails and shovels.

I turned to Matt after they had gotten over the first sand dune. "Well," I said, "I guess we can go now."

"Yeah, we can, uh, go now."

"Matt, this is silly. What are we so scared of? Nothing really happened to us the first time we went in there. Besides, I was in the cabin all by myself this morning, and I didn't have a bit of trouble. If that evil-looking man was going to do anything, he would have done it while I was here alone. Right?"

"Yeah, I guess so."

I made the thumbs-up sign. "Then let's get going."

Matt copied me and pressed his thumb to mine. We grinned at each other and headed for the fort.

With Matt carrying a dim flashlight we'd found in the cabin, we crept into Battery Backus, our very own fort. The cool darkness surrounded us. I shivered again as I remembered our first journey through this door.

Matt turned on the flashlight and began slowly scanning the room. I immediately felt much better.

The room, enclosed with bare walls made of ground-up seashells, was empty. There were no skeletons, no ghosts, no boogeymen—no nothing! Just some old paint cans and other trash lying around.

"What do you think?" Matt asked. "Want to see what's in the next room?"

"Yeah," I answered with new bravery. "Let's go. There's got to be more than this."

We walked through room after room, but, except for a few metal bars that reminded me of a jail, there was nothing exciting to see. Just trash, paint cans, and boarded-up windows.

"Grief!" I said as we came out on the other side of the fort. "Nothing. This fort is nothing but a bunch of empty rooms."

"Well," Matt said, "I guess we couldn't expect them to leave cannons and bombs here for us to play with."

We stood on the hot sand outside the fort and laughed at ourselves. After a few minutes in the scorching sun, I said, "Well then, we'll just have to make up our own mystery about the fort."

"Hey, that's a good idea."

"Okay," I said. "We can pretend that you're the captain and I'm coming to give you a secret, coded message about Blackbeard's buried treasure in the fort." I pointed my finger away from the fort. "I'll come from that side, and—"

Matt looked in the direction I was pointing and froze. I jerked my head to follow his stare. There, on the other side of a hedge, was a huge, dark, rickety, old house hidden in a forest of long-fingered trees. It looked just like a haunted house from an old movie.

I quickly pulled my hand down to my side and looked

at Matt. He was still staring at the house.

"Do you think it could be . . . his house?" Matt asked, his voice shaking.

"I don't know." I ran to the hedge and peered between the small, oval leaves. "Look, the mailbox says SOLOMON GREY. Sounds like it might be him."

"Well, if it is him, he needs to change his name to Solomon *Black*," Matt said. "That would fit him a lot better."

I wasn't in the mood for joking. I started thinking out loud instead. "There isn't a car in the driveway, so he probably isn't home. I bet we could peek in that window by the door. Maybe we can find out something about him."

Matt rolled his eyes and shook his head. "Here we go again."

I led the way as we crept through the bushes. The window was low and easy to reach. With both our faces pressed to the glass, we searched Solomon Grey's kitchen.

"Refrigerator, stove, sink," Matt said. "Oo-oo. Real spooky."

"Don't get smart," I said.

With his hands hooded around his face, he continued to study the kitchen.

I turned my attention to the den. At first glance, things seemed normal there, too. By the window there was a wooden desk with a computer and an old soup can full of pens. There were books scattered all over the desk and on the floor. Then I looked closer at the books.

"Oh, no. Matt, listen!" I started reading the titles out loud. "*Charleston Murders, Deadly Doses, Cause of Death, Crime and Retri . . . Retri. . . .*"

"Retribution!" Matt shouted. "It's Retribution! Do you know what that word means? It means getting even! His books are about murder and getting even!"

My head couldn't tell which end was up, and my ears were ringing like church bells. We had to get out of there!

I spun around and slammed right smack into a brick wall—a human brick wall! Down I went! From the sandy ground, I stared up into the black eyes of the evil-looking man.

My mind started racing. *Will my parents ever find my body? Who'll play first base on the ball team after I'm dead? Oh, I'll never get to sing on TV!*

He reached his hand down toward me, but I scooted back on the ground, keeping my eyes locked with his. Matt stood frozen with his back against the window.

"I'm not going to hurt you," the dark man said. His deep voice sounded as evil as he looked. He reached his hand down toward me again.

That's when I saw his weird thumb. It was short and stubby—and real wide. I looked over at the other hand. Four fingers were stuffed into his jeans pocket, but sticking out of the top was the other thumb. It looked exactly the same.

"I said I won't hurt you," the man said again.

But I didn't move a muscle. I sat perfectly still on the gritty, white ground, afraid to say a word and afraid not to. Matt stood as still as a statue.

"What's your name?" the evil-looking man asked.

I hesitated. What should I do? I finally answered, "Bitsy. Bitsy Burroughs."

"Well, Bitsy," the man said, "you know you shouldn't be peeping in windows—that's against the law. And you really should stay away from that fort, too. It could be dangerous, you know."

Dangerous? Did he say the fort could be dangerous? What about *him*? *He's* the one who could be dangerous!

"Now, you two just go on back home and forget about buried treasure." He stepped back to let us by.

How did he know we had been talking about buried treasure? My stomach jumped into my throat as I realized the only possible answer to that question. He had been spying on us!

Matt dropped the flashlight, zoomed by me, and disappeared through the bushes.

Seconds passed as I sat on the ground alone, trying to decide what to do next. Finally, I took a deep breath, stood up slowly, and brushed myself off. Then I bent over and picked up the flashlight. The evil-looking man watched my every move.

As I took the first step to leave, his big hairy arm shot out in front of me again. It reminded me of a gate with his huge fat thumb for a latch.

"Remember," he said, "stay out of trouble."

With a force I never knew I had, I pushed the hairy gate out of the way and ran with all my might. By the time I reached the sidewalk, Matt was almost in tears.

"Are you okay, Bitsy?" he said. "Are you okay?"

"Yeah, I think so." I put my hands on my head and tried to slow down my breathing.

"Can you believe it?" Matt said. "And did you get a load of those thumbs? Are they deformed, or what?"

"I don't know, but they sure are weird—just like him."

"You said it."

My heart was just beginning to slow down when I heard, "Bitsy! Matt!"

I stiffened, but before I could say anything, Matt yelled, "Hey, how are y'all doing?"

I followed Matt's gaze across the street. Whew! It was just Billy and Tim calling from their front porch.

"We're doing fine, thank you. Just fine," Billy yelled as he rocked back and forth. "Thanks again for the crabs. They sure was good!"

"Oh, you're welcome," I answered quickly before Matt had a chance. Then I grabbed my cousin's arm and started toward the beach. "Come on. Let's tell Mother and Daddy what happened."

"Are you crazy? Are you gonna tell your mother that we were peeping in windows? That's against the law, remember?"

"Oh, grief!" I plopped myself on the sidewalk. How do I keep getting myself into all this trouble? I sat on the hot cement, hugging my knees, folding and unfolding the dimple in my chin.

Jumping back to my feet, I grabbed Matt's arm again

and said, "I've got it. Just let me do the talking."

I dashed down the path to the beach, with Matt right behind me. Mother and Daddy were comparing the tans on their right sides and left sides as Matt and I tumbled onto the towel beside them. I told them part of the story, that we had met an evil-looking man near the fort. Then I described his thumbs.

"Well, I'm sure he was just as surprised to see you as you were to see him," Daddy said. "But since you can't tell about someone by how they look, you need to just stay away from strangers."

Then Daddy squinted his eyes, looked around mysteriously, and whispered, "You know, I've heard of those thumbs."

I could hardly answer. "You have?"

"Yeah. They're called . . . murderer's thumbs."

"They're called what?" I croaked.

"Robert," my mother said.

He laughed at me as I looked at Matt's ghostly white face. "It's okay, y'all," Daddy said. "It's just a folk tale—you know, a legend. The story is that those short, powerful thumbs could crush a man's throat. But of course, it's not true."

I jumped up from the towel and started pacing. "How do you know it's not true?" I yelled. "How could you possibly know? We might be next door to a murderer right this very minute!"

Mother pushed herself up to her feet. "Okay. That's enough. Robert, cut it out. I don't know what to think of you, scaring the kids like that."

"But, Mother—" I started.

"But, Ruth—" Daddy began.

"No 'buts.'" Mother looked at each one of us, including Daddy. "Now," she continued, "everybody stop this silliness and pack up. It's time to think about some supper."

Nobody said a word as we headed back up the path to our cabin. Billy and Tim smiled at us from their front porch as we filed through the screen door. I smiled back and waved. Maybe Mother and Daddy didn't take Solomon Grey seriously, but I was thankful Billy and Tim did.

CHAPTER · 5

"I KEEP FORGETTING, which side are we supposed to put the TanTone on?" Matt asked the next day. He reached into my Cherokee bag for the baby bottle half full of homemade suntan lotion.

"The right side," I answered. "I've told you that a thousand times. Just remember, 'TanTone is right for you!' Get it? '*Right* for you?' It goes on the right side."

"Oh, yeah," he said, nodding his blond head. "Hey, maybe your daddy will let us make the commercials for him. We could be TV stars!"

Matt jumped up from the towel and, holding the baby bottle of greasy lotion, started dancing around while he sang off-key. "If you want the right tan, done the right way, in the right time, use TanTone. I did, and look at me!" He ended with his hand holding up the baby bottle of lotion, his head leaning over against it, and the silliest fake smile on his face. It was obvious he would never make it on TV.

"I hate to tell you, Matt, but if you want Daddy to let

you be in his commercials, you'd better not let him hear you sing!" With that, I took off running across the hard, wet sand, leaving empty footprints in my path.

Matt tried to catch me, but I was too fast for him. I circled back around and collapsed on the towel, completely out of breath. Matt was puffing right behind me.

We were still laughing at his silly commercial when we saw Billy and Tim coming down the path. "Hey," I yelled. "Come on over!"

They looked at each other, smiled, and headed for our towels. I could tell they were glad we invited them.

"Y'all want to help test Daddy's suntan lotion?" I asked after they had settled beside us.

"Sure," they answered together.

"Be glad to," Billy added.

"Good! 'Cause we've got something to tell you!"

While Billy and Tim put on the lotion, Matt and I told them about finding Solomon Grey's house on the other side of the fort. "And when we looked in the window," I continued, "we saw books about murder, and crime, and—"

"And retribution!" Matt said.

I gave him the evil eye for interrupting me.

"What's ret . . . retri. . . ," Tim said.

"Retribution," I jumped in. "It means getting even." I looked at Matt and smiled. I had just gotten even with him for interrupting me.

"Wow!" Billy said. "No wonder y'all was worried. There really is something weird about that guy."

"Yeah," I agreed. "But we can't get anybody to listen to us."

"Well, we're listening, and we believe you. Don't worry," Billy promised, "we'll look out for you."

It was good to know we had friends at Tybee Island who took us seriously.

After a while, Billy and Tim decided the TanTone side was much darker than the Bronzetone side. On the way back to their cabin, they stopped to tell Daddy their results, and he just beamed with pride.

I still couldn't tell any difference. And I was getting a little worried. Can you be in a commercial to sell something if you don't really believe it works better? Would that be lying?

Matt and I were seeing who could blow the biggest bubble gum bubbles when Mother called us in for lunch. Since we were the last two on the beach, we started to gather all the buckets and shovels and sandy towels. I was facing the fort, shaking the sand out of Ann's towel, when I saw him.

I dove to the ground.

"What are you—" Matt started.

"Shhh!" I reached up and grabbed his leg. "Get down!"

He fell down beside me as he whispered, "What's the matter with you?"

"He just came out of the fort."

"Who?"

"Solomon Grey."

"What?" Matt said out loud.

"Be quiet!" I said through gritted teeth. "Solomon Grey just came out of the fort."

Matt sighed and his shoulders drooped. "What could he possibly be doing in there?"

"I don't know, but I bet it's why he doesn't want us to go in the fort." I paused for a moment. "I bet he's afraid we'll find something."

"Find what?" Matt asked. Then he smiled. "I know what it is." He leaned over and whispered in my ear, "He's afraid we'll find a valuable paint can."

"Funny," I said as I wrapped a brown curl around my finger. A thought was forming in my head. "I've got it. I bet it has something to do with buried treasure!"

Matt rolled over on his back in the wet sand and looked up at the sky. "Oh, brother, I don't like the sound of this."

As soon as lunch was over, Matt and I were standing at the cool, dark doorway of the fort. This time I had the flashlight. "Now, remember," I said, "if either one of us sees anything unusual, we'll still stick together. None of this running off and leaving each other. Got it?"

"Yeah, sure." Matt had the little kids' sand pail in one hand and the shovel in the other. He was turning his head constantly, looking over his shoulders. "Got it."

I led the way inside the fort, directing the light into every corner of the first room. "Looks clear here. Now let's get down to business." I held the flashlight in one hand and bent down to start sifting through the trash with the other hand.

"Bitsy!" Matt yelled.

I stood up quickly, my heart playing ping-pong in my chest. "What? What's the matter?"

"You're not really going to rummage through the trash with your bare hands, are you?"

"Yeah. So?"

"So, what about snakes or . . . or spiders . . . or rats! Remember *rats*?" Matt asked, emphasizing the word.

"Of course I do. But right now I'm trying to find some buried treasure. Remember *buried treasure*?" I gave him the evil eye. "Now, are you with me or not?"

He let out a big breath. "Yeah, I'm with you."

But memories of the rat did make me change my mind about my bare hands. I passed the flashlight to Matt, grabbed the plastic shovel, and started digging through the trash. Matt stood perfectly still, holding the light and looking over his shoulder while I shoveled.

"Nothing in here," I said after a few minutes. "Let's go to the next room."

The next room was the same. And the next. Finally we came to the last room, the one that opened next to Solomon Grey's house. I was moving the shovel around in the mess when I hit something hard.

Clunk!

I looked at Matt. Matt looked at me. Then we both looked down at the dirty floor. Carefully, I moved the trash around with the shovel while Matt tried to focus the light on our mysterious object.

Clunk! The sound echoed again through the empty room.

Leaning the shovel against the wall, I slowly squatted down to the filthy floor and stared at our buried treasure. It was a small metal box, covered with dark, peeling paint. It had a rounded top, like a chest—a miniature treasure chest. There was a huge dent in the back, right under the hinges, causing the edges of the box to overlap. I could tell there was writing on top, but I couldn't make out the words in the dim room. I reached up, grabbed the flashlight from Matt's hand, and shined it directly on the box.

Squinting to read the letters, I caught a glimpse of the toy shovel as it started to slide down the wall.

Screech-ch-ch! Boom!! The shovel fell against the paint cans and crashed to the floor.

It was like watching the rerun of an action movie as Matt zoomed passed me again and flew out the door of the room. I could hear his feet slam against the cement floor until he was all the way out of Battery Backus.

"Don't even think about getting any of this buried treasure!" I yelled after him. Grief!

I turned back to the metal box, my hand shaking slightly as I reached to bring it closer. Studying the painted letters again, I read slowly, "W . . . H . . . I . . . T. Whit . . . M . . . A . . . N. . . . " I started laughing out loud. "Wow! This is some buried treasure—Whitman's chocolate candy."

Well, at least it looked like an antique. Maybe it was worth some money. I decided then and there that if it was worth anything at all, I was not sharing it with Matt.

I sat down on the grimy floor and pulled the rusted box onto my lap. Holding the flashlight with my chin, I aimed it at the box as I opened the round top of the chest.

At first glance, I thought it was empty. Then I realized there was something inside. My hand started shaking again as I reached for the yellowed piece of paper at the bottom of the box.

Readjusting the flashlight with my chin, I read the scribbled words:

If buried treasure be what ye seek,
Then ye must work to find it.
Instructions shall be given thee,
But ye must look behind it.

For three steps north and three steps south
And three steps east begin it.
But three steps west and then ye find
That ye are still within it.

It was suddenly very cold in Battery Backus. I read it again, my breath rushing to keep up with my heart. "We found it!" I whispered to the empty fort. "We found instructions to the buried treasure!"

In one motion I dropped the Whitman's box, jumped to my feet, and sprinted out of the fort with the paper.

"Matt!"

Matt and I crashed into each other at the door of the fort. My words tumbled out faster than he could hear them.

"It says three steps north, but I'm not sure which way is north! . . . And we're within it! . . . It's old enough for—"

"Hold it!" Matt demanded, grabbing my shoulders, his face only inches from mine. "What in the world are you talking about?"

"The treasure! I found instructions to the treasure!"

Immediately, Matt pressed his hand over my mouth and jerked his head around, looking for Solomon Grey.

"Are you crazy?" he whispered directly in my ear, his hand still over my mouth. "Do you want him to hear us?"

"MUPHRN!" I tried to speak, but the words couldn't come out.

"Do you promise to be quiet?" Matt whispered, still covering my mouth.

"MUPHRN!"

He moved his hand.

"I said move your hand, and I mean it!" Standing on the sidewalk, breathing hard, I glared at Matt. Neither one of us said a word.

Then I remembered the paper, now crumpled in my dirty hand. I grabbed my cousin by the shirt and pulled him over against the cabin. Then I held on to him as we slid our backs down the wall and sat on the hot sidewalk.

After straightening out the wrinkled paper, I handed it

to Matt. I watched his eyebrows raise and his jaw drop as he read the same words I had read just moments before.

"You mean . . . there really is a buried treasure?" he said.

I smiled and nodded my head.

Then Matt started sounding like my mother. "First of all, the fort wasn't even here when Blackbeard was burying his treasure. Second, somebody else would have found it by now if it was that easy to find. Third, Whitman's wasn't around—"

I stood up, put both hands on my hips, looked down at Matt, and patted my foot on the cement. He stopped listing his excuses.

I jerked the secret code from his hand. "If you don't want to help, that's fine. I'll find it myself." Then I folded my arms across my chest and added, "Just leaves more for me."

With that, I turned to go back into Battery Backus and was startled to see Billy and Tim at the edge of the sidewalk.

"Hey, what're y'all doing?" Billy asked, glancing from me down to Matt and back up to me again.

Now, I'll be honest here. I didn't really mind sharing the treasure with my favorite cousin, Matt. But there was no way I was gonna let Billy and Tim in on the deal.

"Oh, nothing," I said. "Uh, Matt and I were just going in to help Mother with supper, and, uh, I'm going to eat it all up if he doesn't come help me!"

Matt sat on the sidewalk and grinned that silly, fake

grin. Believe me, he has absolutely no acting ability.

I grabbed his arm, pulled him to his feet, and led him toward the cabin door. "See y'all later!" I called over my shoulder.

We watched out the window as Billy and Tim walked back across the road to their house. I don't know if it was my imagination or not, but it sure looked like they were arguing.

C H A P T E R · 6

"HURRY UP, KIDS!" Daddy yelled as Matt and I were finishing the supper dishes. I still hadn't figured out why everybody thought Ann was too young to help clean up the kitchen. I sure remember standing on a chair and drying dishes when I was her age. But of course, when I was her age, I didn't have a big sister to do all the work. Grief!

Daddy came to the doorway of the kitchen. "Aren't y'all about through? The rest of us are ready to go stargazing."

You see, we had been to the Wednesday night service at the Chapel-By-The-Sea, and the pastor had talked about how God had created the universe. So Mother and Daddy decided we should all go out that night, climb up on top of the fort, and look at the stars.

Matt and I wanted to work on our secret message, but my parents thought we needed some family time. Personally, I thought we'd had plenty of family time that week. What I needed was private time. But, I decided I would do what they wanted and call it "keeping the peace" time.

Anyway, Matt and I grabbed a couple of blankets, and we all headed for the fort. After we climbed up on the flat roof, we spread out the blankets and settled on our backs. With all of us gazing up at the black sky, Daddy pointed and started explaining.

"Now, first of all, look right up there. See that group of stars that looks kinda like the water dipper Grandma Burroughs has hanging on her wall? That's actually called the Big Dipper."

"I don't see it, Daddy," Lynn said.

"Me, neither," Ann said.

"There are seven stars," Daddy continued. With his finger he outlined the pattern. "See the handle, and then the dipper part, and—"

"Oh, I see it," Matt said.

"Where?" I asked, hitting my cousin in the side with my elbow. "I can't find it."

Daddy pointed again and said, "I'll keep my hand right here. You slide over and look right up my arm and follow it into the sky. See?"

"Yeah, I see it," I said. "Hey, it really does look like a water dipper."

Daddy pointed over a little farther. "And there's the Little Dipper. Some people say it looks sorta like the big one, only upside down and smaller."

"I found it!" I announced first. "But it's harder to see."

"Yep, I got it," Matt said.

"Me, too!" said Ann.

"Me, too!" said Lynn.

Yeah, right, I thought. *Sure you did.* But I didn't say anything.

Then Daddy started rattling on and on about stars and how you couldn't see all of them all year round. My mind wandered back to the treasure and the secret code. If only I could figure out those directions. . . .

Then my mind jumped back to the present when Daddy said something about "north."

I sat up quickly. "What did you say, Daddy?"

"Oh, you mean the part about Ursa Minor and—"

"No, no," I interrupted. "The part about finding which way is north."

"Oh. I just said that you can always find out which way is north by following the Little Dipper up to the end of the handle. That last star is Polaris, the polestar. And it always points you in the north direction. It has guided sailors and their ships for centuries."

Well, I didn't really care about sailors or ships. All I knew was that star could guide me to the buried treasure tonight. I whispered my great idea to Matt.

But he wasn't interested. "Forget it," he whispered. "If you think I'm going with you back inside this fort tonight in the pitch-black dark, you are crazier than I thought."

All I said was one word. "Chicken!"

I wasn't exactly excited myself about going in the fort at night. But we could still figure out where to start. So when Mother and Daddy decided it was time to go back in, I begged Mother to let us stay out a little longer. Matt gulped.

"Okay," Mother agreed. "But don't stay out too long, and don't go anywhere else."

We watched my family as they gathered the other blanket and headed back to the cabin. When we were sure they were out of earshot, we both started talking at once.

"There's the polestar, and—" I said, pointing.

"If we come back first thing in the morning—" Matt was saying.

"Okay, okay, wait a minute," I said, putting up my hands to stop the conversation. "Now that we know which direction is north, we'll come back first thing in the morning and get started."

Matt stared at me. "That's what I said."

"Well, it's settled, then. Now let's see if we can find any more of those Draco stars Daddy was telling us about."

Matt and I stretched back out on the top of the fort, gazing at the stars and listening to the quiet. We must have been there about fifteen minutes when I heard a noise.

"What was that?" I whispered loudly.

"What was what?" Matt sat up.

"Shhh!" I put my finger up to my lips and pulled him back down. "Listen."

Then I heard it again and looked at Matt. When I saw his eyes almost pop out of his head, I knew he had heard it, too.

There it was again! And it was coming from Solomon Grey's house! Slowly, we scooted like army men toward the edge of the roof until we could look down into Mr. Grey's backyard. We watched for a moment while our brains took in what our eyes were seeing.

There he was. The big, dark, evil-looking man was digging a hole in his backyard. A huge burlap sack full of something was piled beside him on the ground.

I was afraid Solomon Grey could hear my heart pounding as we watched him dig and dig and dig. Neither Matt or I said a word. The man kept digging until the hole was so deep, he had to jump in and shovel the dirt over his head.

We watched silently as Mr. Grey climbed out of the hole and started pushing the heavy sack, first with one foot and then with the other. Then we watched as he bent down and, with both hands, forced the heavy, unknown object into the hole. It landed with a loud *plop!*

That's when I knew it was a body.

C H A P T E R · 7

IT WAS THE MIDDLE OF THE NIGHT, hours after everyone else had gone to sleep, before Matt and I could settle ourselves down. We couldn't agree whether or not to tell my parents about Solomon Grey and the dead body. Personally, I figured that since they hadn't taken us seriously yet, they wouldn't be concerned about this, either. I was sure they would have a good reason for Mr. Grey to bury a body in his backyard.

Something like, "Well, it is Wednesday, you know. The cemetery doesn't bury people on Wednesday." Or maybe, "I'm sure it was somebody who just didn't want to pay his death taxes, so nice Mr. Grey helped them out." Right.

But anyway, it seemed like we had just gotten to sleep when somebody started pounding at our door. "Mr. Burroughs, are you in there? Mr. Burroughs? Open up, this is the police!"

I knew immediately why they were there. *We were right! It's barely light outside and the police have already found out about Mr. Grey and the buried body!*

I heard Daddy get up and put on his robe. By the time he got to the door, we were all gathered around him.

I reached up, tugged on Daddy's sleeve, and smiled knowingly to the group. "I am well aware of why the police are here," I announced.

Daddy opened the door to see two police officers in blue uniforms standing on the sidewalk. "Are you Mr. Burroughs?" the lady officer asked.

"Yes," Daddy answered slowly.

She tucked a strand of long blonde hair behind her ear. "I'm Officer Phillips and this is Officer Teague. We're from the Tybee Island Police Department."

Then Officer Teague spoke up. "Do you have a daughter named Bitsy? Bitsy Burroughs?"

Here it comes, I thought. *Now I'll get my recognition for knowing that Solomon Grey really is an evil man. I wonder if there'll be a reward. Everybody will be so impressed!*

I squeezed by Daddy, pulled back my shoulders, took in a deep breath, and answered proudly, "I'm Bitsy. And I know why you're here."

Well, let me tell you, that's when things fell apart. The police officers said something about somebody writing on the fort with paint, and messing up a landmark, and having to pay for damages, and staying out of the fort.

"Wait a minute! Hold it! Time out!" I yelled.

But it was too late. The next thing I knew, I was standing with the two police officers and my family in front of Battery Backus. We were staring up at the words, "BB

WAS HERE," scrawled on the wall of the fort. The paint was still damp, dripping down the cement wall.

"I didn't do it. I promise," I cried. But nobody was listening. I looked at Mother, my face begging for her to believe me. But she just stared at me with wet eyes and then turned her head away.

I ran over to Daddy. "Daddy, I didn't—"

But he interrupted me. "Get in the cabin, young lady. We'll talk later."

Sobbing, I walked back to the cabin, keeping my eyes on the ground. I reached for the screen door and then stopped to take one last look at my parents talking so seriously with the police officers. My sisters were hiding behind my mother, watching all the activity with frightened eyes. Matt frowned and shook his head in disbelief. Then I saw Billy and Tim across the street, leaning against their fence, the blue lights reflecting off their faces. At least I knew they would believe me.

After the police officers left and we all were back in the cabin, I realized Mother and Daddy knew I was innocent. The problem was, they couldn't figure out who did it, either.

Matt and I told them about seeing the evil-looking man bury something in his yard, but—just like I expected—they figured there was a reasonable explanation for it.

"That's what I meant when I said I knew why the police officers were here," I said. "I was talking about Solomon Grey. Believe me, we would never mess up Battery Backus. It's our very own private fort."

"Well, kids, it's not anymore," Daddy said. "The police officers agreed that if y'all scrub off all the paint and don't go back in the fort, they won't file any charges."

"Don't go back in the fort? But, Daddy—"

"I don't want to hear another word. It's final. When the stores open up this morning, I'll get some turpentine. You and Matt will scrub off the paint, and then you'll stay out of the fort."

I knew better than to say anything else.

"Well, it could have been worse," I said, dipping my brush back into the pail of stinking turpentine. "They could have made us march around the lighthouse with heavy weights on our backs like they did in the olden days."

Matt tried to laugh, but it was hopeless. "Some vacation," he mumbled, wiping a sweat trail off the side of his face. "I don't have to work this hard at home."

I stared at my cousin. I couldn't believe he would say that to me after all I had done to give him a free vacation. "What about me? Do you think I'm enjoying this? Now, let's quit arguing and try to figure out what happened. Who did this? And why did they use my name?"

Moving the scrub brush up and down with each word, Matt answered, "I . . . don't . . . know. . . ."

"Need any help?" We turned around to see Billy and Tim walking toward us from across the street.

"Thanks," I said, brushing a brown curl out of my eyes. "But the police officers said we have to do it." Then

I looked at our friends with the most sincere face I could make. "You believe us, don't you? You know we didn't do this, don't you?"

"Course we do," Billy said. "We knowed y'all wouldn't mess up the fort."

Tim nodded and smiled, his toothless grin shining. "But who did do it? And why?" he asked. That was the most I had ever heard him say.

"That's what we want to know," I said. Then I began to list the facts. "Well, first of all, we know the little kids couldn't have done it, even though I'm sure Ann would love to get me in trouble. Nobody else knows my name except y'all . . . and Solomon Grey. . . ." My mind suddenly started playing leapfrog! "And Solomon Grey doesn't like us—especially after he caught us peeping in his window!"

Billy nodded his head. "Hmm, that's true."

"Yeah," I said. "Boy, I wish we'd never even gotten close to that window. I guess we just got all caught up in the mystery of the evil-looking man and weren't thinking straight." I stared at the ground and watched my feet do nothing.

Then I looked up at our friends and said, "But anyway, we know there's something fishy about the fort and Solomon Grey."

"Yeah," Matt said. "He even told us himself to stay out of it. And that was before we saw him bury a body in his backyard."

"A body?" Billy whispered.

Then we told them about Solomon Grey and his secret burial ground.

"Well, there's your answer!" Billy shouted, snapping his fingers. "Don't you get it? What better way to make you stay out of the fort and away from him than to get you in trouble with the law?"

Matt dropped the scrub brush. "Of course! Of course—he did it to make sure we couldn't go back in the fort or hang around his house."

Billy nodded his head. "Yep. I think that's it. And if I was you, I think I'd stay out of that fort. Otherwise, he'll just get y'all in trouble again."

"You're right," I answered sadly.

"Well," Billy said, "if y'all are sure we can't help, we'll head on back. Sorry about all your troubles."

"Thanks," Matt and I said together. We watched them cross the street and go back into their cabin.

I leaned against the turpentine-covered wall, folding and unfolding the dimple in my chin. Something was trying to get into my brain. But what was it?

Then it hit me. "Matt, I've got it! Solomon Grey doesn't want us in the fort because he doesn't want us to find out that there really, truly, honestly is buried treasure in there! And . . . and maybe that poor person in his backyard is there because he found out about it!"

Matt's blue eyes were like saucers. He didn't say a word as he thought through the idea.

"Yeah!" he finally shouted. "And Solomon Grey wants to find it first. He wants it all for himself."

"Be quiet! Do you want everybody to go looking for it? Now let's get to work and finish cleaning this wall so we can figure out a way to find our treasure."

It took us all day, but we finally got every drop of paint off our fort. It didn't matter what anybody said, Battery Backus would always be *our* fort. And by the end of the day, we knew that Solomon Grey was the one who should have scrubbed the wall. Solomon Grey was the guilty one.

Matt and I were anxious to work on our plans for finding the treasure, so we weren't interested when Mother tried to get us to play Monopoly after supper.

"But you're good at it, Bitsy," Mother said. Then she whispered in my ear, "And you're the only one who can give me any competition."

That made me feel really good, but Matt and I had more important things to do. How could I think about playing a game when we had a murderer next door? A murderer who had framed us for messing up the fort. A murderer who was looking for our buried treasure. Why couldn't Mother understand how serious this was?

We went into the bedroom and Matt climbed up on his bed. I pulled my Cherokee bag out from its hiding place behind the chest. Dumping the bag on the bed, I fumbled through a zillion bubble gum balls and broken crayons, looking for the directions to the buried treasure.

When I found the yellowed, crumpled paper, I climbed up on the bed beside Matt. Then I read the instructions out loud again. ". . . ye must work to find it . . . instructions shall be given thee . . . but ye must look behind it. . . ."

That's when it hit me. "Behind it? Matt, that's it!" I shouted, jumping up and down on the bed. "We've been thinking it was inside the fort, but the treasure is *behind* it." I turned a flip on the bed while Matt checked the sheet of paper.

"I think you're right," he said.

I stopped jumping and stared down at my cousin. "Of course I'm right. Tomorrow we'll start digging behind the fort." I stared out the window toward the mysterious house. "And there's not a single thing Solomon Grey can do about that."

CHAPTER · 8

THE NEXT MORNING, Matt and I woke up early and got to work. It was really hard convincing Mother to let us go anywhere near the fort. But we assured her we were not at all interested in exploring Battery Backus anymore. "Cross our hearts and hope to die, we won't go inside," we promised.

That made my mother laugh. "Okay, okay. You don't have to go that far. I believe you. Just be sure you stay away from that fort. I don't want you touching a single cement block."

We promised again, this time without hoping to die. Then we headed out the door. I hate to admit it, but Matt was the one who figured out that the treasure wasn't just behind the fort, but it was in the sand dune. I'm sure I would have figured it out if I had gone to the museum with my family.

At the museum, Matt had learned that back in 1897 the soldiers piled huge mounds of sand between each fort and the ocean. That way, the enemy ships couldn't even see the forts from the water. It just looked like great big sand dunes piled high on the shore.

And now we knew that Battery Backus's great big sand dune was hiding buried treasure, just for us.

"Okay," I said, standing on top of the dune, looking at Solomon Grey's house. "The polestar was this way."

Matt shook his head. "Um, nope. I don't think so." He faced the ocean and turned left. "It was more this way."

"No way."

"Bitsy, I hate to be the one to tell you, but you don't know everything. Now I'm telling you, it's this way."

"Well, go right ahead, Mr. Smarty Britches. Since you think you know so much, you just go right ahead and find the treasure." I plopped down on the sand and turned up my nose while Matt continued to shake his head.

Then I heard him plundering through my Cherokee bag. After a minute he sat down on the sand and pulled the bag onto his lap. I didn't say a word.

"Okay, where is it?" Matt finally asked, looking up from the bag.

"What? Where's what?"

He stood up roughly and ran over to me, accidentally kicking dry sand in my face. Spitting the gritty stuff out of my mouth, I jumped up and faced him, my hands balled into tight fists. Eyeball-to-eyeball we stood, taking in deep breaths as we stared each other down.

I was the first to crack a smile. Then I couldn't hold it in any longer. I laughed, bending over and holding my stomach.

Matt joined in and put his arm around my shoulder. "Okay, okay," he said between laughs. "I admit it . . . you do know everything." He smiled and grabbed my shoulders. "Now, where are the directions?"

I smiled. "Right where I knew they were." I reached into my pocket, pulled out the paper, and waved it in the air.

It didn't take Matt but a second to grab the piece of paper from me and start reading. "Okay. It says, 'If buried treasure be what ye seek—'"

"I know I'm seeking it," I interrupted. Then I smiled. "How about ye?"

"Cut it out, Bitsy. Now, listen. 'Then ye must work to find it. . . .' Well, we're sure working," he said. "And then it says, 'Instructions shall be given thee, but ye must look behind it. . . .' We've already figured out that part."

Snatching the paper, I said, "Now this is the part I'm confused about. All right, let's face *your* north." I grinned at Matt, turned toward the ocean, and then a little to the left. I started reading. "'Three steps north. . . .'" We took three steps. "'And three steps south. . . .'" We turned around and took three steps. We were back where we started. "'And three steps east begin it. . . .'" We turned left and took three more steps. "'But three steps west and then ye find—'"

"We find we're exactly where we started!" Matt said, throwing himself to the ground.

I dropped down beside him. "Grief!"

We sat there for a while, just looking out at the white-capped ocean. Finally, I got tired of sitting, doing nothing. I stood and brushed the dry sand off my clothes. "Well, one way to be sure we don't find it is not to look!"

"What? What in the world are you talking about?"

"What I mean is, we can be sure we won't find anything if we don't look for it. You can sit here and pout if you want to, but I'm digging."

I threw the first shovel full of sand as Matt stood up. "I'm not pouting," he said, reaching for the pail.

We took turns. First I shoveled for a while and Matt dug with the pail. Then we traded. We had been working for at least thirty minutes with nothing to show for it when Matt forced the shovel down into the sand. "I'm going back to the cabin for something to eat. How about you?"

"Nah, not yet," I said, looking up from my kneeling position in the sand. "You can bring me something if you want." I stood and stretched my back, then reached down and picked up the toy shovel. "We could probably get a lot more done if we had a real shovel."

"I hate to tell you, Cousin, but I don't think it would make any difference," Matt said. "I've 'bout decided we're wasting our time out here."

"Party pooper!" I yelled as I watched him walk carefully down the back of the steep sand dune and head toward the cabin. I jumped into the small pit Matt had been working on and, with all my strength, pushed the shovel deep into the sand.

Clunk! The shovel vibrated in my hands while my heart vibrated in my chest.

I stood perfectly still, waiting for something . . . I didn't know what. Listening for something . . . I didn't know what.

I tried the shovel again. *Clunk!*

Slowly I slid to my knees, dry sand falling back in with me. I watched as my shaking hand stretched toward the object, remembering the last time I had reached into the unknown. I felt something hard and cold. My breath came in short bursts of air as I erased the sand from the top of the round, tan treasure.

It was almost like a rock—a hollow, rounded, smooth rock with holes in it. Frantically, I dug around the object with my hands and then watched as white sand fell silently through the two larger openings—the openings that were staring up at me.

And then my mind screamed as the words rushed through my mouth. "A skull!"

I fought my way out of the pit, fell back in, and fought my way out again. I couldn't catch my breath, and my head was turning cartwheels as I scrambled across the top of the sand dune and fell down the other side. I screamed, but nothing came out. I tried again. Nothing! No sound. No squeak. No scream.

Where is the cabin? Where do I go? I couldn't think. Then I saw the familiar white cement block building. It seemed to be running from me as I tried to reach for the door. I grabbed the handle and fell across the doorway. The last thing I remembered was Matt yelling, "Aunt Ruth!"

When I woke up, Daddy was leaning over me, cradling my head in his hands. "Bitsy . . . Bitsy," he whispered, leaning down to kiss my forehead. "It's all right."

Then I remembered the skull and sat straight up in bed, the darkness starting to close in on me again. I felt a cool cloth across my face and opened my eyes to see the darkness disappear as my mother sat beside me.

"It's okay, Bitsy. It's okay," Mother said, taking my hand in hers.

"But what about the skull?" I cried. "What about the dead person?"

"The police are here," Daddy said. "And so is Dr. Shaw, that doctor I found for your mother. They're digging up the area right now and trying to figure out what's going on."

"But we know what's going on," I shouted. "We know it's Solomon Grey. We know—"

"No. We don't know, Bitsy," Daddy interrupted. "We don't know anything. After the police are finished, we'll tell them what you and Matt saw and that's all. But you don't *know* anything."

"I want to go out there. I want to see what they're doing," I said as I started to get out of bed.

Mother put out her arm to stop me. "No, Bitsy. You need to stay in here with us. The police want everyone to stay out of their way."

"But that doesn't mean me. They'll want me out there to show them—"

"No," Mother answered sternly. "We're all staying

right here. They'll come when they want to talk to you."

I crawled out of the bed and walked over to the bed-room window. I gasped. I couldn't believe it. But there, right in front of everybody, was Solomon Grey.

"There he is!" I screamed. "He's right there!"

Solomon Grey turned toward me and smiled.

C H A P T E R · 9

THAT NIGHT we had the quietest supper ever. Ann didn't jabber on and on about waves or sand or crabs, and Lynn didn't spill her milk or throw her food or wet her pants. Mother and Daddy just kept looking at each other and then glancing at Matt and me out of the corners of their eyes. I was sure they wanted to say something, but nobody said anything.

We had just finished eating when we heard a knock at the door. I jumped up to answer it, but Daddy held his hand out as he slid back his chair.

"Stay here till I call you," he said, and then he headed for the door.

I heard the squeak of the screen door as it opened. Then I heard several voices, but I couldn't understand what they were saying. Finally, Daddy called, "Bitsy. Matt. Come on in here."

I was out of my chair and across the room before Matt had even stood up. *Oh, brother!* I thought. *Please don't let Matt go chicken on me now!*

"Hurry up, Matt," I whispered loudly. "This is our chance to prove we're innocent."

We walked through the door to find the two police officers and another man in the room with Daddy. "Bitsy, Matt, this is Dr. Shaw. And you've already met Officer Phillips and Officer Teague."

"We sure have," I mumbled.

Daddy gave me a "mind your manners" look and continued, "They want to talk with you and ask you some questions. Don't worry, I'll stay right here with you." Then Daddy turned to the lady officer. "Go ahead."

Officer Phillips cleared her throat. "Well, first of all, your daddy tells me that you two saw something the other night that you would like to tell us about."

I glanced at Matt to see if he wanted to talk first. He just sat there, staring at the floor. He didn't move a muscle. No chance that he was going to say anything.

"Well," I started, "Wednesday night Matt and I were on top of the fort, looking at the stars, when we saw Solomon Grey in his backyard. He was, um, burying a body."

Nobody said a word for a moment. Then Officer Phillips spoke up. "Now, let me get this straight," she said. "You say you saw Mr. Grey bury something in his backyard? And you think it's . . . a body?" She turned to Officer Teague and smiled.

That's when I got mad. "We did see it! Why won't anyone believe us?" I cried as I ran over to Daddy.

"Officer," Daddy said, "I'm a little surprised at your

response. Don't you think it's worth at least looking into?"

"Yes, I'm sorry, Mr. Burroughs. It's just that, well, Mr. Grey has been here for as long as I can remember. We know him really well. I just can't imagine that—"

"I see," Daddy said. "And since we're visitors on the island, then naturally we're the ones who are wrong."

"No, sir. It's just that with the problem Bitsy has had in the past with the fort—"

"But I didn't have a problem! I've tried to tell you that, too." I turned to Daddy for support. "I didn't do it. Tell them, Daddy."

"Officers, I can assure you that Bitsy and Matt did not paint the fort. I can also assure you that if they say they saw Mr. Grey burying something in the backyard, then you had best look into it. Now, is there anything else?" Daddy asked, cutting the visit short.

"I would like to say something." We were surprised that Dr. Shaw had spoken up. "I know I wasn't involved in the episode with the fort, so I can't say anything about that. But I do know that I have just spent all day digging up a skeleton. . . . A complete . . . skeleton," he added, emphasizing each word to the officers. "One which, I might add, we wouldn't even know about if it weren't for these two children here."

Then he turned and faced Matt and me. "Children . . ."

I hate it when grown-ups call me a child. I am twelve years old, you know.

". . . believe me, I'm taking you seriously. So seriously

that another officer and I are leaving for Atlanta tonight with the skeleton you found. We're taking it to some special people there who can tell us what happened. I want to thank you personally for your help."

Then he looked over his shoulder at the officers. "Maybe you shouldn't jump to conclusions so quickly." Facing us again, he put out his hand. I reached out and shook it. Then he stepped over and shook Matt's hand. When he finished, Dr. Shaw walked across the room. With his hand on the screen door, he stopped and said to the officers, "I'll see you when I get back from Atlanta."

It was completely quiet for several seconds after Dr. Shaw left. Then Officer Phillips cleared her throat. Finally she said, "I'm sorry for the misunderstanding, folks. It's just that we never have any problems around here, and this has been quite a day for us."

"Tell me about it," I muttered under my breath. Daddy squeezed my shoulder, and I got quiet.

"I understand," Daddy said. "But it's been quite a day for us, too."

"Yes, well, we'll be on our way," Officer Teague said. "And I promise you, we'll look into your story, Bitsy. We'll be back in touch tomorrow."

Daddy walked with them to the door while Matt and I just sat there on the couch.

"Did they really believe us?" Matt asked.

"I don't know," I answered. "But we'll find out tomorrow when we see if they question their old pal Solomon Grey."

C H A P T E R · 1 0

IT WAS EVEN HARDER to get to sleep that night than it had been the night before. Could it really have been just two days since we had seen Solomon Grey bury a body in his backyard? That seemed like years ago, so much had happened. But finally Matt and I ran out of steam and fell asleep.

I was dreaming that my Bobby-Cat was scratching my bedroom screen at home. "Stop, Bobby-Cat!" I screamed in my dream. "Stop!" But he did it again.

Then my eyes jerked open. It took a minute for the fog to clear from my head before I could remember where I was. I held perfectly still in the dark silence. Then I heard it again. And this time I was awake! I held my breath, trying to quiet my heartbeat, but it was hopeless. My heart continued to announce every beat to the world.

"Bitsy," a voice whispered into the blackness.

I became a statue while my heart pounded a thousand times a minute. Only my eyes moved as I scanned the room for the intruder.

"Bitsy." There it was again—coming from the open window.

I didn't move. I didn't breathe.

"It's us—it's Billy and Tim."

I finally let the old air out of my lungs and took a deep breath of fresh air. My heart still yelled each beat. Slowly, I inched my body out of bed and put on my robe. I looked around the room, which was dimly lit by the streetlight. Matt was snoring on his bed. Ann and Lynn were a mass of tangled arms and legs on theirs.

"What are you doing out there at this time of night?" I asked when I reached the window.

Billy was standing alone on the sidewalk. "Sorry to wake you," he said, "but I knew you'd want to know."

"What? Want to know what?"

"He's doing it again."

"Who's doing what again?"

"Solomon Grey. He's digging in his yard again, and . . ."

I held my breath.

". . . I was sure you'd want to see."

"No!" I whispered loudly. "I don't want to see! I've seen enough! Just go get the police!"

"The police?" Billy said. "By the time we get all the way over to the police station, he'll be finished."

"But I'm already in enough trouble. Besides . . . I'm afraid of him."

"Listen, Bitsy, we don't have much time. I . . . I have a camera, and . . . and we could take pictures. Then if he gets away, we have proof."

I leaned my face against the window screen and peered out into the darkness. "Where's Tim?"

"He's around the other side of the fort, keeping an eye on Solomon Grey for us. Now, get Matt and come on before it's too late."

My heart and my mind started a battle with each other. In my heart I knew that Mother and Daddy wouldn't want me to go out in the middle of the night, especially after what we'd already been through. But my head was filling with thoughts of all the glory we would receive when we caught Solomon Grey red-handed. I could see the headline: TWO TWELVE-YEAR-OLDS SAVE TYBEE ISLAND FROM MASS MURDERER. We'd probably get a reward and have our pictures in the paper. We'd be famous! And, best of all, it would clear my name. Besides, Billy would be there to help.

My mind won the battle.

I whispered to Billy, "Okay. We'll be there in a minute. Just meet us at that light pole over there." I pointed behind him.

"Great." He took off for the meeting place.

In a few seconds I was dressed and standing at Matt's bed. I stared at my favorite cousin and shook my head. Convincing him to go was going to be a tough job. Taking a deep breath, I reached across his bed and gently touched his arm.

"What?" he yelled, sitting straight up. My hand covered his mouth instantly, as I jerked my head around to watch my parents' room. Thank goodness, I didn't hear any movement in there.

"It's me," I whispered in his ear. "Now, be quiet."

Eyes as big as yo-yos glared at me in the darkness. I turned back to watch the doorway to the bedroom. He mumbled something under my hand.

I whispered again. "When you're quiet, I'll move my hand."

He mumbled again, softer this time. I let go.

"Are you crazy? What are you doing?" he asked quietly. Then he noticed my clothes. "And why are you dressed?"

I started pulling on his arm. "Come on, hurry up. Solomon Grey is at it again, and this time we're gonna catch him."

"You *are* crazy. I'm not going anywhere with you—it's the middle of the night." Then he raised the sheet and tunneled himself under it.

"Matt, don't give me a hard time," I begged through the cover. "Billy has a camera, and we can take pictures of—"

"Why can't we be like normal people and just call the police?" Matt said, his voice muffled by the sheet.

"First of all, we don't have a telephone here. And anyway, he'd be long gone before we could ever get all the way over to the police station and back again, that's why. This way we can catch him red-handed, pictures and all."

Matt didn't say anything.

"Now, hurry up and get dressed while I check on Mother and Daddy."

Matt still didn't answer, but he slowly pushed the cover

back, lugged himself out of bed, and started searching his suitcase for clothes.

I tiptoed to the door between our bedroom and my parents' room. With my eyes now adjusted to the darkness, it was easy to see Mother lying on her back next to Daddy. Both of them were snoring. But neither one was stirring. I turned back to our room. Matt was ready.

I motioned with my finger for him to follow me as I took the first few steps into my parents' room. The only sounds were the snoring duet by Mother and Daddy and the constant hum of the fan blowing across them. Matt was one step behind me by the time I reached the screen door. I reached up to place my hand on the door and suddenly stopped. The instructions to the treasure!

I held up my hands to Matt, signaling him to stay put, and headed back toward the bedroom. I was glad to see Ann and Lynn still jumbled like tangled spaghetti, still sound asleep. I squeezed behind the chest and grabbed the sturdy handle of my Cherokee bag. Throwing the bag over one shoulder, I returned to the front bedroom to find Matt waiting right where I had left him.

Carefully I unlatched the screen door, once again hearing the *boom-boom, boom-boom* of my heart.

I gently pressed against the door. *Cr-re-ea-ak!*

We stopped immediately, with the door half open. I could see Billy hiding behind the light pole at the edge of the street. Matt's ghostly white face glowed in the dark. The snoring duet continued behind us.

We tried again. *Creak!* Shorter this time.

I took a deep breath and tried again. Silence.

Just as we got outside the door, Matt whispered, "What in the world did you bring your bag for?"

"Don't you see? This is our chance to get some answers. While Solomon Grey's explaining this mess he's gotten himself into, maybe he can also explain the mysterious instructions to the buried treasure. That's probably what he's been looking for anyway. Who knows—that might be why he killed all those people to begin with."

We reached the streetlight, and Billy said, "Well, I see y'all made it."

"Yeah, well, I still don't like it," I said. "But if it will stop this evil murderer and clear my name, I guess it's worth it. Now, where's the camera?"

"Oh, Tim's got it over on the other side of the fort. He's probably already got some real good pictures. Y'all take the lead and watch ahead. I'll guard the back of us. Come on, let's go."

I looked back at the dark, quiet cabin. No sign of life. I glanced up and down the deserted street. Nobody in sight. I decided we needed to laugh. "Well, it looks like the only people crazy enough to be up at this time of night are a crazy murderer and the crazy people who are going to catch him."

Nobody laughed.

Matt and I walked carefully down the sidewalk. As we passed the fort, we noticed the odor of turpentine still hanging in the air. Billy followed behind us.

"Y'all hurry up," he said. "Somebody's gonna see us."

"Well, that would be okay," Matt said. "We'd just get them to run to the police station while we took the pictures."

"Of course!" I said, slowing down as we reached the bushes next to the fort. "Why didn't I think of that? That's what we should have done in the first place, Billy. Matt could go wake my parents and let them get the police while you and I take the pic—"

In an instant there was a rope around Matt and me, squeezing us together, forcing out our breath. Round and round the rope went. Tighter! Tighter!

"What—" I started.

"Shut up!" Billy commanded, reaching for the long, wide pieces of tape already torn and stuck to a light pole.

"Billy—" I started again, but I was stopped as he pressed the tape over my mouth.

"This will shut you up!" he said.

I fought with the rope and screamed through the tape as Billy covered Matt's mouth. Matt fought uselessly for a moment and then stood still.

After he checked the knots and the tape, Billy started pulling us toward the fort. We pulled against him, trying to lead us back to the cabin, but Billy was too strong.

As soon as we were inside the fort, Billy took his end of the rope and tied it to one of the bars in the last room, the room next to Solomon Grey's house. Then he pushed us to the floor. I felt the round gum balls under me as I landed hard on my Cherokee bag.

We watched in the dim light as Billy squatted down,

reached into a tattered grocery sack, and pulled out a flashlight. He turned on the light and held it with both hands under the edge of his chin. The light shining up across his face gave him an eerie glow.

Then he spoke. "All right. Now just tell me where it is, and I'll let you go. It's as simple as that."

What was he talking about? Did he mean the treasure? Tell him where the treasure was? That was simple enough. We didn't have any idea where the treasure might be.

I tried to tell him through the tape that we couldn't find the treasure, but he immediately put his finger to his lips.

"Shhh. Let me finish. Then I'll take off the tape so you can tell me everything. Now, first of all, I need to know where your hiding place is—where you've got our money hid. If it's all there and none of it's missing, I'll let you go—if, and this is a big if—if you promise not to tell nobody about this. Ever."

Money? What money? I tried to tell him again under the tape that we had no idea what he was talking about, but he grabbed my chin and shouted through clenched teeth, "I said to let me finish!"

Then he continued, "When you promise not to tell nobody, that means *nobody*. Not even your parents. Got it? And believe me, I'm watching you. And I'll be watching you for the rest of your life. So don't you ever think you can get away with telling anybody. Now, are you ready to talk?"

I nodded my head violently and made a muffled

sound. I'd been ready to talk! Matt just sat there. I think he was in shock or something.

Keeping the flashlight shining under his chin, Billy reached up with one hand and pulled a tiny section of tape from my lips.

Talking out of a corner of my mouth, I finally said, "I don't know what you're talking about. What money? What hiding place?"

The flashlight crashed to the floor as he reached up with both hands and forced the tape back over my mouth. "You brat!" he yelled. "Don't play games with me! I know you found our money in the fort. So cut it out! Now, I'm giving you one more chance. Are you ready to get serious? 'Cause I'm serious as a heart attack!"

I nodded again, and he removed the tape a second time. "Please believe me, Billy," I pleaded. "The only thing we found in the fort was the secret code to buried treasure, I promise! And we still haven't been able to find the treasure!"

It wasn't what he wanted to hear. Jumping to his feet, Billy reached into the grocery sack and pulled out a roll of wide tape. In a flash, he rushed behind me and wound the tape completely around my head.

"We worked so hard to get that money from the restaurant," he said as he added more and more tape. "Did you really think you could get away with stealing it from us?" Then he reached up and loosened the rope.

"Okay. You wanna play games?" he said as he sat back down on the floor. "I'll show you how I play."

Reaching into the sack again, he pulled out a piece of paper and a pencil. Then he turned to me and smiled. He reached for my right hand and pulled it out of the loosened rope. I knew now not to fight him.

After placing the paper on the floor in front of me, Billy put the pencil in my hand and said, "Now write what I say."

Then he started dictating. "Dear Mother and Daddy." Suddenly he stopped, bent down, and looked at me, his sour breath turning my stomach. "And I know what you call your parents, so don't try anything smart like writing 'Mom and Dad.' Just write exactly what I say."

I did as I was told. Matt just sat still, his eyes glazed over, looking off in space somewhere.

Then Billy continued dictating, "Gone exploring. Don't worry. Be back soon."

I recorded his message word for word.

"Okay. Let me see." He took the paper from the floor and checked it. "Good," he said, replacing the paper. "Now sign it 'I love you, Bitsy.'"

I stopped. My hand shook and my heart quickened. I looked up at Billy.

He grabbed my hand and pressed it onto the paper. "Do it! Do it now! Put 'I love you, Bitsy.'"

I quickly wrote the words he had dictated. When I finished, he jumped up and ran behind me again, pulled my arm back under the rope, and retied the knot.

He stood above us and smiled. He looked pleased with himself. He grabbed the paper from the floor and headed for the doorway. "Now don't try nothing funny. It'll only take me a minute to stick this in the cabin door." And then he was gone.

I turned to Matt. He was still lost in outer space somewhere. I leaned over and rubbed my shoulder against his and tried to say his name.

"Mmm" is all that came out. I tried again. "Mmmm." When I tried to talk, it just sounded like humming. That's when I got the idea to sing to him, even though I couldn't say the words. The problem was, the only song I could think of at the time was "There Shall Be Showers of Blessing!" Can you believe it? Blessings? Ha! What a joke!

Anyway, I started humming that old church song, and soon I was praying new words with the tune.

"Lord, please don't let Billy kill us.

"Please make this a promise of God.

"Let all the evil ones leave us,

"Sent away by the Father above."

Matt blinked. He blinked again. Then he turned to me and answered, "Mmmm." After a few seconds, Matt started humming, too, but, as always, he was off-key.

I stretched my stiff arm behind me and brushed across his hand with my fingers. Even though his mouth was taped shut, I could see Matt trying to smile.

In a few seconds we heard Billy's pounding footsteps and stopped humming before he appeared in the doorway of the fort. Our fort. Battery Backus. He crossed the room in three giant steps and untied the rope from the bars. Jerking us up from the floor, he threw the rope over his shoulder and started to pull.

"Come on!" he yelled. "You had your chance!"

Billy led the way as we left the fort and started down the sidewalk toward the road. We struggled behind him, stumbling over each other's feet.

And with each stumble, I could feel the Cherokee bag thump against my back. I shifted my arms around, stretching until my hands could touch the special bag and try to hold it in place. It was comforting to feel the round, hard gum balls inside. *If only I could get one to my mouth,* I thought. *It sure would taste good.* I started wiggling my mouth to loosen the tape.

"Quit dragging!" Billy shouted, pulling harder on the rope.

Where are we going? Where is he taking us? Then I refocused my thoughts and moved the gum balls between my fingers, trying to inch one up to the top. Little by little, the bubble gum was guided by my aching fingers up the side and to the edge of the open bag. Ah! I got one in my fingers!

I had loosened the tape on my mouth a little bit. Now to get it to my mouth. Matt watched as I arched my head back and around and pushed my hands up through the ropes. I raised my shoulders to bring my arms higher while sinking my head as deep into my neck as possible. But nothing would work. I couldn't get the bubble gum to my mouth.

Giving up, I relaxed my shoulders and stretched my

fingers back toward the open bag. But I didn't make it. I cringed as the gum ball slipped through my fingers. Matt and I stared as it bounced like a tiny golf ball on the sidewalk behind us. We looked up at Billy, but he didn't seem to hear anything.

I felt like we were Hansel and Gretel. Then I stopped. Hansel and Gretel? Hey, it might be corny, but it might just work!

Billy pulled on the rope. "Come on!" he demanded.

We took a few stumbling steps but kept our eyes on Billy. He still didn't act like he heard anything.

Within seconds, I had another gumball up to the edge of the Cherokee bag. When it was safely in my fingers, I dragged my foot slightly to cover the sound of the bubble gum dropping to the sidewalk. Then I got to work on the next one. And then the next one. All the way to the lighthouse.

CHAPTER · 11

MATT AND I STOOD at the huge base of the giant light-house and stared up at its black-and-white form.

"Lucky for me they don't have lighthouse keepers any-more," Billy said. He tried to turn the locked doorknob. "Great! Guess we'll have to go in through the window." He pulled on the rope again and dragged us to the window on the side of the lighthouse.

We stood there helplessly as Billy threw a rock and shattered the glass, the noise echoing through the quiet night. After breaking out all the glass, he picked up the rope and started pulling again.

"Come on! Get in there!" Billy commanded as he pushed us through the hole.

We crashed to the cold cement floor together. Billy climbed in right behind us.

Matt and I struggled to stand, tripping over each other as we tried to do as we were told.

"All right. This is your last chance," Billy said. He reached into his back pocket and pulled out . . . a knife!

We both tried to scream, but the tape held back our voices.

Billy laughed. "Did I scare you?"

Matt and I both nodded our heads really fast. Billy grinned and walked toward us. I screamed another silent scream and then shut my eyes as tight as possible and held my breath. I felt Billy's grimy hand touch my face as he tugged on the tape covering my mouth.

Snip! The knife sliced through the tape.

I started breathing again. Then I cringed as Billy pulled the tape from my skin and jerked it from my hair. Tears stung my eyes, but I was determined not to let him see me cry.

"Like I said, this is your last chance." He untaped Matt's mouth and pushed us toward the winding staircase. "Now get on up there! You have until we get to the top of the lighthouse to tell me what you did with that money. And if you don't, well, it's bye-bye Bitsy and Matt!"

Then he started to laugh. "And the wonderful part is, the police will think you just fell from way up there because you was trespassing again. Just like with the fort—trespassing and exploring! Ha, ha!"

I couldn't believe what I was hearing. "But you know we didn't paint the fort! Solomon Grey did it, remember? You said so yourself!"

Billy grinned. "Wrong!"

"What?"

"You goofed!"

"What?" I asked again.

"Don't you get it? It was me and Tim! We wanted you to stay out of the fort and stay away from our money."

I didn't understand. "Billy, what are you talking about?"

"You're serious, aren't you? You still don't get it, do you? See, me and Tim, we're the ones your daddy read about in the paper. We're the ones that robbed Williams Seafood. Then we hid all that money in the fort. That's why we had to paint your name on the fort. To keep you outta there."

He stopped a moment and shook his head. "And to think we thought the money would be safer in the fort than it would be in the cabin with us." He squinted his eyes. "Well, it would have been safe if you nosy little brats hadn't come along." Then he bent down and whispered right in my face, "Now, for the last time, tell me where it is!"

"But we *are* telling the truth, Billy!" I cried. "Why won't you believe us?"

"I'll tell you why! I'll tell you why I don't believe you! Because the money's gone, that's why!" he yelled. "Nobody else knew it was there except me and Tim and—"

"And that's all!" I interrupted. "You and Tim! We sure didn't know anything about it!" Then I looked around. "Where is Tim, anyway?"

"He's done gone to Savannah to buy us bus tickets for the getaway. My job was to stay here and watch the money. But when I went to check on it, it wasn't there. It was gone because you took it." He shook his head.

"You done messed me up, messed me up bad."

Then he glared at me. "And I'm gonna mess you up—mess you up bad if you don't tell me where that money is. You got a hundred and seventy-eight steps." He pushed us. "Now get started."

We were still tied together, but we tried to do what Billy said and started up the stairs. After only one step I lost my balance and fell hard, bringing Matt down with me. Blood from my scraped knee dripped onto the metal step.

This time it was Matt who spoke up. "Billy, we'll never make it to the top like this. Please undo the ropes. We promise we won't try anything."

"Well," Billy said, rubbing his chin. "Okay. We'll try something else." He pulled the knife out again. I held my breath, but it only took a few strokes for the knife to slice through the rope. It fell into a pile at our feet. Then Billy closed the knife and put it back into his pocket. That's when I finally breathed again.

He reached down and picked up one of the larger pieces of rope. "Put out your hands," he demanded.

We did as we were told. Then he tied my left wrist and Matt's right wrist together and held the other end of the rope in his hands as he stood behind us.

"Okay. Get back up," he said when he was finished. "Now that's the last stop we're making. You two better start a-walkin' and start a-talkin'."

We struggled to our feet and headed up the steps. Nobody said anything for a while, and I started thinking about my parents. *Do they know we're gone yet? Will they know the message isn't true? Will someone find the bubble gum?* "Oh, God," I prayed, "please help us."

One hundred and seventy-eight steps is a long way up. Billy was out of breath after just a few flights of stairs, but Matt and I were doing fine.

"Billy?" I said.

"Yeah?" he answered, huffing and puffing behind us.

"I'm confused. What about Solomon Grey? Where does he fit into the picture?"

"I . . . I don't know." He stopped to catch his breath on the step below us. After a few seconds he laughed. "Me and Tim don't know nothing about him. But y'all was scared of him, so we just figured we could use it to help us." Then he smiled. "It worked, didn't it?"

"Yeah, it sure did," I said. "But what about the grave in his backyard, and the skeleton, and the books on his desk? And why would he tell us to stay out of the fort?"

Billy stood a few seconds more, still trying to catch his breath. "Can't figure that one out. But you was right—he is weird."

"BITSY! MATT!" A voice echoed from the stairs below.

Billy pushed us. "Get going!" Then he reached for his knife. "And keep your mouth shut!"

We quickly started up the steps again.

"BITSY! ARE YOU IN HERE?" That voice. Where had I heard it before?

And then it hit me. *Oh, no! It's Solomon Grey!*

"Grief!" I yelled as I grabbed Matt's arm. "It's him!"

Matt and I took off up the stairs, pulling the rope out of Billy's hand. We ran faster than ever, leaving Billy behind us, gasping for air.

We raced up the lighthouse steps. Matt screamed, "What's he doing here?"

"I don't know," I answered as we took the steps two at a time.

"GET BACK HERE!" Billy called up the stairway.

We were still ahead of Billy, but even I couldn't last long at this rate. My legs weighed two hundred pounds apiece, and it felt like I was breathing through a straw.

After about ten circles around the stairs, I gave out. "We've . . . got to . . . slow down," I said, leaning against the cold cement.

"Yeah," was all Matt could answer as he slid down the wall and sat on the metal step.

We could hear the *clank-clank-clank* of the men's footsteps below us. Their voices were far away now, but we could still hear both of them calling our names.

"As long as we're this far ahead, I think we can rest a second," I said. "Can you believe it—two bad guys trying to get us at the same time?"

"Yeah," Matt said. "And what did we ever do to them?"

Before I could answer, Solomon Grey's voice echoed up the staircase. "HEY BILLY, YOU LEAVE THOSE KIDS ALONE!"

Matt and I just stared at each other. "What did he say?" Matt said.

"STAY OUT OF THIS, MR. GREY," Billy yelled

back. "THIS AIN'T GOT NOTHING TO DO WITH YOU. IT'S BETWEEN ME AND THEM." His voice was closer now.

We took off again. Up the lighthouse steps. Higher! Higher!

"HEY, KIDS . . . JUST . . . TELL ME . . . WHERE . . . IT IS," Billy shouted, taking a breath after almost every word. His heavy footsteps echoed through the lighthouse. "I'LL LET . . . YOU GO . . . BACK HOME . . . AND WE'LL . . . JUST FORGET . . . THE WHOLE THING . . . OKAY?"

But Solomon Grey shouted, "KEEP RUNNING, KIDS! I'VE ALMOST GOT HIM!"

Mr. Grey didn't have to worry about us . . . we weren't gonna stop running! After all, we were running from both of them!

Then another voice called from far, far below, "BITSY! MATT!"

Could it be? It was! It was Daddy!

We stopped. Matt and I stared at each other. *What do we do now?*

Then Daddy called out again, "BITSY, ARE YOU THERE?"

"DADDY!" I cried. "PLEASE HURRY! THEY'RE TRYING TO GET US!" Before I knew what I was doing, I started back down the steps, dragging Matt behind me.

"Bitsy, wait!" Matt begged. "We're gonna run right smack into Billy this way!"

"I'M COMING TO GET YOU, BITSY!" Billy called, much closer than before.

"KEEP RUNNING, KIDS! YOU CAN BEAT HIM!" Mr. Grey shouted.

Daddy, too far below us to hear what was going on, called again, "BITSY! MATT! WHERE ARE YOU?"

I looked at Matt. He looked at me. The questions just hung in the air. What should we do? Our silent discussion was cut short as a battle erupted below us.

"E-R-G-G-H!" *Crash!*

Matt and I took one last look at each other and knew what we had to do. The sounds of feet clanging on metal steps and fists hitting human flesh rang up the winding staircase as we headed down toward the action.

I don't know what I expected to see when we got there, but I was shocked as we rounded the last curve. Solomon Grey, the evil-looking man, had Billy pinned to the cold cement wall. Billy's knees were bent, with half of his body pressed back against the lighthouse steps. Mr. Grey's black, piercing eyes were inches from Billy's. His thick fingers and short, stubby thumbs were wrapped around the robber's neck. His murderer's thumbs!

"Mr. Grey, don't kill him!" I cried.

But it was too late. Billy's body suddenly relaxed as his hands released their hold on Solomon Grey's hair and dropped to the floor. The evil-looking man stood tall and gasped for breath. He towered above Billy's lifeless body. My scream echoed through the huge lighthouse like a chorus of bats.

Daddy was there before my scream ended. He ran past Mr. Grey and stumbled at the step below us, grabbing me and Matt in his arms as he fell to the stairs. He cried into my shoulder.

And the police were right behind Daddy. They immediately reached down to Billy, forcing handcuffs on his limp wrists.

Tears stung my eyes as I said, "You don't need to do that. He's dead."

"Dead?" Officer Phillips said. Then she smiled. "No, he's not dead. He's just passed out." Then she turned to the evil-looking man. "Good job, Solomon. Guess all that mystery-writing stuff paid off, huh?"

"What?" I asked, pulling away from Daddy as he stood up beside me. "You mean Billy's still alive?"

"Yeah," Mr. Grey answered. "I just used a little trick I discovered while I was writing my last book."

Matt and I both stared at the evil-looking man. I spoke first. "You mean you're not a killer?"

Mr. Grey's bulky body shook with laughter, and he rubbed his black beard. "Me? A killer? What makes you think such a thing?"

Then Matt jumped in. "Well, because you've got books about murder on your desk. And . . . and what about that body you buried in your backyard?"

Solomon Grey shook his head and smiled. "First of all, the books are reference books. You know, for research. I can look up all kinds of things about crime and murder in those books and then use them in my stories. I'm a writer."

Matt looked at me. But this time I kept my mouth shut. "Okay," Matt said slowly. "So . . . what about the body? We did see you bury a body, you know."

"I can answer that one," Officer Phillips answered. "We spoke to Mr. Grey after you kids told us about the grave in his backyard. Come to find out, you're right. He did bury a body in his yard."

"See, I told you—" I started.

Officer Phillips interrupted, "The body of a Great Dane."

"A what?" Matt said.

"A Great Dane," Mr. Grey said. "A dog. My mother lives in a condo here on the island, and she had two pets, two enormous Great Danes. Have you ever seen one?"

I shook my head.

"Well, they weigh more than you do. They weigh about the same as a small adult. Anyway, she loved those dogs so much that when one of them died, she couldn't bear to have Dr. Verdin just get rid of it. He's the vet, you know."

I nodded my head.

"So she asked me to bury it in my backyard. That way, she can visit the grave anytime she wants to. You can come see it tomorrow, if you like. I've even made a marker for it."

We didn't say anything for a few seconds. Finally, Matt spoke up. "Well, what about the skeleton in the sand dune?"

"Uh-h," Billy moaned from the floor.

We all jumped.

"Just stay put," Officer Teague said, holding Billy down with his foot. "You're not going anywhere."

"Yep, Billy," Officer Phillips said. "Looks like we're gonna be seeing a lot of each other for a while."

The police officers placed themselves on either side of Billy, reached down, grabbed his arms, and helped him to his feet. He wobbled between them.

Then Billy's eyes focused on us. I hugged Daddy tighter, and Matt held on to his other side. Daddy shivered between us.

"You kids really don't know nothing about the money?" Billy asked.

Neither one of us said a word, but we both shook our heads.

"What money?" Officer Phillips asked.

"The restaurant money," Matt answered quickly. "Billy told us that he and Tim robbed Williams Seafood last week."

"Well, I'll be dogged," Officer Teague said. "You two not only found a skeleton, but caught a robber, too! Been quite a day for you, hasn't it?"

"I'll say," Matt answered.

"Sure has," I said.

The police officers supported Billy as he stumbled down the steps, shaking his head in disbelief, headed for the jail.

Then I remembered. "But wait. What about the skeleton?"

"Go on and tell 'em about that, Solomon," Officer Phillips called back over her shoulder. "And kids, we'll talk first thing in the morning and get the whole story from you."

We turned to Mr. Grey.

"Well," he said. "Dr. Shaw called the police station from Atlanta about midnight. Looks like it didn't take the specialists long to figure out that skeleton was real, real old. Probably a soldier from one of the wars. Nobody could believe how you two kids found it after all these years."

Daddy sat back down and sighed, folding and unfolding the dimple in his chin. He looked up thoughtfully at Solomon Grey and then reached out to shake hands with him. "So you really are a good guy, aren't you?"

Mr. Grey laughed. "I like to think so," he said. He led the way as we all started down the lighthouse steps.

I finally spoke up again. "Well, thank goodness you're a good guy. And thank goodness you came along when you did. But, how did you know we were in trouble?"

"To tell you the truth, I didn't know. The officers were out patrolling the island, saw my lights still on, and stopped to tell me about Dr. Shaw's phone call. We stood outside and talked for a while, then decided to check out your cleaning job on the fort."

Solomon Grey smiled. I didn't.

"Anyway, after they left, I got to thinking about you two finding that skeleton." Then he laughed. "I even started planning how I could use it in my next book."

"But how did you know Billy had us?" I asked again.

"Oh, I'm sorry. I was getting to that part. Anyway, I had started back toward my house when I saw lights come on in your cabin. Then I heard your mother calling—you know, calling your names."

"Yeah," Daddy interrupted, "that's when we came outside looking for you kids and found the note you wrote. But your mother and I knew right away that something was wrong. We knew you would never write 'I love you' instead of '143.'" Daddy hugged me tight.

Solomon Grey continued the story. "Then they ran over to ask if I had seen you two. While they were explaining everything to me, I thought I heard breaking glass, coming from this direction."

I interrupted, "That must have been when Billy threw the rock in the window downstairs."

"And then about that same time your sisters walked up, chomping on all that bubble gum!"

"Well," Daddy said, "actually it was Ann who found the bubble gum. She shared it with Lynn."

"Wait a minute!" I held up my hands to stop everyone on the steps. "You mean my bratty little sister, Ann, found the trail of bubble gum?"

"Yep, sure did," Daddy said.

"And it really did work? You really did follow the bubble gum balls?"

"Yes, Bitsy," Mr. Grey answered.

Daddy nodded his head and smiled. "Me, too."

"Cool," I said. "Corny, but cool."

Mr. Grey continued, "And, if you'd let me, I'd like to put that in my next book, too." Then he slowly rubbed his bushy beard. "But I have a feeling I've read that little trick somewhere before."

I smiled at Mr. Grey and looked over at Matt. "Can you believe it, Matt? Bubble gum balls! And of all people, can you believe that little squirt found them. Maybe she's not such a bad little sister after all."

Matt agreed. "Nope, not bad at all."

Quietly, we started down the stairs again. Matt broke the silence. "But, Mr. Grey, you still didn't finish the story. How did the police get here? And how did you know what was going on?"

"Well, since I knew the island better than your parents, I figured I could follow the gum balls and find you easier. So I sent your dad for the police while I ran on ahead to see if I could find you."

"And you got here just in time!" Matt said.

"Yeah, at first I didn't really know what was going on. But I could hear Billy yelling at you, so I knew you were in trouble. All I could do was try to get to him before he got to you."

"And it worked!" I shouted as I jumped off the last step. Then I hugged Solomon Grey. "Thank you, Mr. Grey. Thank you very much."

Matt hugged him too, and we all started down the road back toward the cabin, with Daddy between Matt and me, holding our hands.

In just a few minutes a patrol car pulled up beside us,

and my mother and sisters climbed out. Mother, her face a combination of fear and happiness, waddled in our direction as my sisters ran to us, crying all the way.

I knelt down and hugged my sisters. Then, holding Ann out at arm's length, I looked at her reddened eyes and wet face. "Thank you for being such a smart little sister," I said. "You saved my life, you know."

"Yeah, I know." Then she paused. "And Matt's, too."

I hugged her again. "Yeah, and Matt's, too."

CHAPTER · 12

THE SKY WAS STILL BLACK when we finally got back to the cabin. We were all exhausted, but it still wasn't time to sleep. Not yet.

First, Daddy knelt by the tattered sofa, then Mother struggled to her knees. One by one we filled in the spaces between my parents and bowed our heads.

Daddy led the prayer. "Dear Heavenly Father, thank you, thank you. I can't say 'thank you' enough for protecting Bitsy and Matt tonight. You are so good to us. Lord, please help each of us to live our lives in a way that will honor and glorify you. Amen."

We all said, "Amen."

"Wait a minute, Daddy," Ann said before we could get up. "Wait a minute. I want to talk to God, too."

"Okay, sweetheart, go ahead."

"Dear God, thank you for taking care of my big sister and my cousin. And, God, please help the bad men to not be bad anymore. Amen."

We all smiled and nodded in agreement. "Amen."

* * *

The sun was just coming up when Ann and Lynn climbed into my bed. But this time I didn't complain. This time I was actually thankful for my two little sisters.

Lynn snuggled beside me. "Bitsy, do you think the piwat will come back and get me and Ann?"

"The pirate?"

"Yeah, the piwat that taked you and Matt to the lighthouse."

"Oh, he wasn't a pirate, Lynn. He was just a mean man. And he will never ever come back again to scare any of us, believe me."

"I'll always believe you," Ann said, snuggling on the other side. "You're big."

"Well, I'm not always right, and I don't always do the right thing. But believe me when I say that I'll always, *always* love you." I hugged them both. "I sure am glad you're my sisters." And for the first time, I realized how much I really did mean it.

Matt roused up and called across the room, his voice still raspy with sleep, "Bitsy, what about the buried treasure?"

"Grief!" I sat up straight in bed. In all the commotion and excitement, I had forgotten about the buried treasure.

"Do you think Solomon Grey knows anything about that, too?" I asked. "He sure had an answer for everything else."

Matt jumped out of bed. "I don't know, but let's go find out!"

"Good idea!" I yelled.

"Good idea!" Ann and Lynn copied.

We dressed in no time and ran to tell my parents where we were going. "Okay," Daddy said, "but don't go any-where else."

"You don't have to worry about that!" I said. But as we raced out the door, we crashed right smack into Offi-cer Phillips and Officer Teague.

"Good morning!" Officer Phillips said. "You kids sure are up early. You must have heard the good news."

"What good news?" Matt asked.

"Well, the police in Macon found Tim riding the bus, on his way to Atlanta. And guess what. He had a suit-case full of money." She glanced at Officer Teague and back down to us. "Looks like he was running out on his friend Billy."

"You mean Tim took the money out of the fort, and Billy didn't even know anything about it?" I asked.

"Yep. Cheated his own friend. Guess it just proves you can't trust a bad guy, even if he's your friend."

"Yeah, we thought he was *our* friend, too," I said. "Sure can't tell by looking at people, can you? And here we thought it was Mr. Grey we had to be afraid of."

The police officers laughed. "So where are you headed in such a hurry?" Officer Phillips asked.

Matt answered. "Well, we were going to Mr. Grey's house. We wanted to see if he had any ideas about how to read the secret message we found in the fort."

"Oh, I see," Officer Teague said. "It does look like

you're pretty busy right now. How 'bout Officer Phillips and I go get some breakfast and come back in an hour or so?"

I couldn't believe what I was hearing. "Would you? Would you come back later?"

"Sure. You can bet Billy and Tim aren't going anywhere. We'll see you in a little while."

Matt and I raced over to Mr. Grey's house, with my little sisters chasing behind us.

Mr. Grey opened the door. "Well, good morning. I'm surprised to see you up so early."

"Well, we've got another question for you," I said.

"Okay. Let's hear it."

Matt butted in, "Do you know anything about buried treasure in the fort?"

Solomon Grey laughed, his bushy beard separating to reveal his open mouth. He didn't look evil at all. "So you did find it," he said.

"You mean the instructions to the buried treasure?" Matt said.

"Yes. I heard you kids talking about buried treasure that day you were peeping in my windows, and—"

"Oh, we are so sorry about that, Mr. Grey," I said. "Please believe me."

He laughed again. "It's okay. Actually, I got a kick out of it, me being a mystery writer and all. As a matter of fact, it was so much fun hearing you kids talk about buried treasure that I decided to help you along."

I was confused. "What do you mean?"

Then he slowly glanced over the neighborhood, stooped down to us, and whispered, "I buried a treasure for you."

"You did?" Matt said.

"Yep. I can say for a fact that there really is buried treasure in Battery Backus," he said. "I buried it there myself."

"All right!" I shouted, clapping my hands. "Let's go get it!"

"Did you find the secret code?" Mr. Grey asked.

"Yes, sir," I said. "We found it days ago. We just couldn't figure out how to find the treasure."

"Well, go get your instructions and meet me at the fort in the same room where you found them."

We took off for the cabin, tugging at the little ones to hurry. Minutes later we were in the fort, holding the directions and the flashlight.

"Okay. What does it say first?" Mr. Grey asked.

I started reading, aiming the flashlight at the mysterious words. "If buried treasure be what ye seek, then ye must work to find it."

"We understand that part," Matt said.

I continued, "Instructions shall be given thee, but ye must look behind it."

"Do you get it?" Mr. Grey asked.

"Sure," I said. "It means look behind the fort. And we did, remember? Mr. Grey, I hate to say it, but a skeleton is not my idea of buried treasure."

He chuckled. "Mine, either. But that's not what it means."

"It's not?" Matt asked. "Then what does it mean?"

"It means look behind the instructions."

"Behind the instructions," I repeated. "Do you mean in the wall behind where we found the candy box?" I asked as I raced to the wall made of crushed seashells. I ran my hands across the rough surface. I didn't feel any openings.

"No, no," he answered, shaking his head. "Read it again."

I started again. "Instructions shall be given thee, but ye must look behind it."

"I know," Matt yelled. "Just what it says. Look behind the instructions."

Solomon Grey smiled. Matt and I raced to the old metal Whitman candy box sitting in the middle of the trash.

I grabbed it first and turned it over. "There's nothing on the bottom of this box."

"Didn't the note say look behind the instructions?" Mr. Grey said.

Matt grabbed the box from my hands and searched inside the bottom. "Wait a minute. I think there's something written here. Shine the light on it, Bitsy." But before I could, he grabbed the flashlight and lit up the inside of the box.

"'Floor.' It just says 'Floor,'" Matt said.

"Floor?" I repeated. "This fort is huge. Does that mean we have to search the entire floor of the fort?"

"Read the next part," Mr. Grey said.

I started reading. "For three steps north and three steps south. . . . Now, wait a minute. We've already done that and you don't get anywhere. When you follow these instructions, you just end up in the same place."

Solomon Grey smiled.

Matt and I caught on at the same time and scrambled down to the floor right where we stood. We ran our hands over the rough cement surface. And there it was. A crack.

Mr. Grey pulled a screwdriver from his back pocket. "You might need this."

Matt took the screwdriver and placed the blade in the crack, barely shifting the thick, heavy piece of cement. I snatched the paper hidden in the crack and waited for Matt to hand back the screwdriver.

"Here, Matt," I said, handing the crumpled note to my favorite cousin. "I'll hold the flashlight. You read."

He stared at me for a moment and then turned his attention to the paper. My heart pounded as he unfolded it and started reading out loud.

"I'm sorry you couldn't find treasure buried by Blackbeard the Pirate, but maybe one buried by Blackbeard the Writer will do." Matt and I both laughed and turned back to the paper. "Come to my house when you find this note, and you will receive the treasure."

I looked up to thank Mr. Grey, but he was gone. "Come on," I yelled, plopping Ann on my hip as Matt grabbed Lynn. "Let's go!"

Solomon Grey met us at his door with four cups of chocolate ice cream.

"Thanks, Mr. Grey," I said as I pulled the paper top off Ann's ice cream. "Chocolate is my favorite."

We were all sitting around the red metal kitchen table, licking the chocolate off our lips, when Mr. Grey stood up and started out of the kitchen. "Excuse me just a minute. Stay right here." After only a few seconds, he returned with even more goodies.

It was just like Christmas! The little ones each got a life-size doll as big as Lynn, and two sets of doll clothes. Matt and I got handheld computer games. Then Mr. Grey handed each of us a Slinky. I had always wanted one, but Mother wouldn't hear of it. She said it was a waste of money for just a piece of curly wire.

We were all on the floor in Mr. Grey's living room, admiring our new treasure, when someone banged on the door.

"Mr. Grey! Kids! Are you in there?" It was my daddy!

Solomon Grey rushed to the door and found Daddy standing there, his mouth gaped open and his eyes about to jump out of his head.

"It's my wife!" he shouted to Mr. Grey. Then he turned to me. "She's going to have the baby!"

I didn't hear another word. I dashed past Mr. Grey and Daddy and ran to the cabin to help my mother.

I jerked the screen door open to find her standing at the bed, calmly packing her suitcase. "Mother!" I yelled. "What are you doing? Aren't you supposed to be in bed?"

"In bed? I'm having a baby, Bitsy, not a heart attack. When your daddy gets back, we'll ride to the hospital."

"But what about Dr. Shaw? He's not here, remember? He's still in Atlanta with the skeleton!"

"Oh, that's okay. They'll have another doctor at the hospital in Savannah."

"Mother, how can you be so calm? You're gonna have a baby!"

She smiled. "I know that, Bitsy." Then she hugged me. "And I hope she's just like you."

I hugged her hard and started to cry. "But what can I do?"

She put her hand under my chin and lifted my face up toward her. "Well, first of all, you can calm down. I'm fine. Everything's fine. But I need you and Matt to stay with the girls while we go to the hospital. Daddy's making sure Mr. Grey will be available in case you need him."

I sniffed and wiped the tears from my cheeks. "Okay, Mother. I can do that." Then I grabbed her clothes and threw them into the suitcase. "Let's go."

I carried her suitcase to the car and watched in amazement as Daddy climbed in the backseat.

"Daddy!" I shouted.

"Robert!" Mother said, shaking her head.

Daddy crawled out of the backseat and opened the front car door. "You'd think I'd never done this before."

Shaking my head, I watched as Daddy pulled the car away from the curb and screeched around the corner. We all stood on the sidewalk in a cloud of dust. Nobody said a word.

Finally, Solomon Grey spoke up. "Well, looks like this

will be a vacation to remember."

"You said it," I said.

"Bitsy," Ann said, "after the baby comes, will we get to be on TV?"

"I don't know, Ann. We'll have to wait and see."

"On TV?" Mr. Grey asked.

"Yes, sir. See, if we have another girl, Mother wants us to be a quartet and sing like those sisters who used to be on television. You know, the Lemon Sisters."

He chuckled. "I think you mean the Lennon Sisters."

"Yes, sir. That's right." I was about to whisper to him that I would rather have a baby brother and just sing by myself, when our car came squealing around the corner. Daddy slammed on the brakes right in front of us.

We watched my daddy jump out of the car and run around the yard like a wild man. He wasn't making sense. "The bridge! The bridge! We can't get off the island!"

I ran to Mother's side of the car. "What in the world is he talking about?"

She answered calmly. "Can you believe it? A barge has crashed into the bridge supports, and they won't let anybody go across until they check it out. We can't get off the island."

"But how are you going to get to the hospital?" I cried. "How are you going to get to Savannah?"

"Well, hopefully, it'll be taken care of quickly."

"But what if it's not soon enough?"

What could I do? I had to help my mother!

"I've got it!" I shouted. "What about Dr. Verdin?"

"What?" Mother asked.

"The veterinarian, Dr. Verdin! Remember, he's just down the road. I bet he could help!"

"Bitsy, be serious—" Daddy started.

But Mother broke in, "Robert, uh, I think we'd better do something—fast."

That was all I needed to hear. I took off running to Dr. Verdin's office. Thank goodness he was there and agreed to help. Within minutes we were back, and Daddy and the vet helped Mother out of the car and into the cabin.

I waited outside with Matt and my sisters and Solomon Grey, and I prayed that my mother would be all right. Inside the cabin, Dr. Verdin, the Tybee Island veterinarian, delivered his very first human baby—Robert Daniel Burroughs.

CHAPTER · 13

NEEDLESS TO SAY, this *was* a vacation to remember. Two days after Danny was born, Williams Seafood Restaurant treated our whole family to a free meal while the newspaper people were there, interviewing us and taking our picture.

It was great! I felt like a movie star or something. On top of that, the food was the best I'd ever eaten. But it didn't last. As soon as we were through with the meal, Mother and Daddy herded us all up and loaded the car to head home.

But my fame wasn't over. When we got back home, I got lots of attention because everybody wanted to hear the story of "What I Did This Summer." And the story was a little better each time I told it. Kids came from all over the neighborhood just to meet me. They wanted to hear the tale of the girl and her cousin who dug up a skeleton, caught a robber, and found buried treasure.

As far as the suntan lotion was concerned, Daddy decided his TanTone was going to make us a million. So he found a company in Charlotte, North Carolina, that made containers for lotion. And that's when he ran into trouble.

He found out it would cost $2,000 just to make the bottles to put the TanTone in. And guess who didn't have $2,000. He tried to convince Mother by saying that the only way to make money was to spend money. But she just reminded him that he didn't have any money to spend. He didn't have an answer for that one.

We never made our million.

Then to top it off, I got a terrible toothache the week after we got home and had to go to the dentist. When he said I had five cavities, Daddy knew I hadn't been following the bubble gum rules. That evening I sat on the couch with a numb mouth full of fillings and watched Daddy carry the box of gum balls out the door. I apologized to my daddy for not following the rules. He said he forgave me, and I know he did, but I never saw the bubble gum again.

Oh, yeah, I almost forgot. After Danny was born, I wrote a letter to the television station to see if they needed a girl to sing all by herself on TV. But I guess I'll have to tell you about that one next time.

Vonda is working on her next book, Bitsy and the Mystery at Amelia Island. *Bitsy heads to historic Amelia Island, Florida, to visit her best friends, Garrett and Ellie. But the children soon discover the abandoned house next door has some dark secrets. Could one of those secrets be a ghost?*

You can learn more about Bitsy and her friends, enter cool contests, and talk with the author! Just ask your parents if you can visit

www.vondaskelton.com

www.silverdaggermysteries.com

Fourteen-year-old Wil Prichard is in trouble. He's picked up an unusual object from an airplane crash site that turns out to be a rare dragon egg. Now, along with his best friend, Amanda "Spunk" Fitch, he's in a race for his life.

Charles Edwin Price, author of *Mystery in the Old Dark Attic*, has written many books of folklore and mystery that are enjoyed by all ages.

People in the small town of King's Creek had always said the grand old Southern manor on Walnut Hill was haunted. Twelve-year-old tomboy Peggy Patrick and her family move into the house and find out that not only is the ghost real, but it's Great-Aunt Matilda!

Mignon Ballard, author of *Aunt Matilda's Ghost*, has so far carefully avoided frightening her five grandchildren with bedtime stories.